Glenn Martin lives in Sydney, although he lived in the bush on the far north coast of New South Wales for two decades. He has been a school teacher, a manager of community services organisations, and a commentator on management, business ethics, employment law and training and development. He has been the editor of publications for management and training professionals and an instructional designer for online learning. On the side he has written over a dozen books.

The Quilt Approach: A Tasmanian Patchwork

Glenn Martin

G.P. Martin Publishing

The Quilt Approach: A Tasmanian Patchwork
By Glenn Martin

Published 2020 by G.P. Martin Publishing
Website: www.glennmartin.com.au
Contact: info@glennmartin.com.au

Book layout and cover design by the author
Typeset in Sitka 11 pt
Printed by Lulu.com

Images by the author. Front cover: Sculpture at Cascades Female Factory,
Hobart, by members of Senior Momentum: a metal rendition of the Rajah
Quilt. Back cover: Sculpture at Cascades Female Factory, Hobart.

ISBN: 978 0 6480811 8 0 (pbk.)

A catalogue record for this
book is available from the
National Library of Australia

The beginning

I went to Tasmania in October 2019. My first visit had been in December 1973. The second time I came better armed with knowledge about the place, and about my ancestors who had spent some years there. Edward Lewis and Sarah Crosby, great great grandparents on my father's side, were sent to Hobart Town as convicts, Edward in 1845 and Sarah in 1850. They met and married in Hobart, and my great grandmother was born in Launceston. After that, everyone in the family comes from Sydney.

I had no great mission, I just wanted to see some of the places they had been, to get a sense of it. Memories are so much tied up with place that their time in Van Diemen's Land, as it was called then, must have remained with them for the rest of their lives. It is not hard to imagine some trace of it running through my veins.

One of the places I went to was Cascades Female Factory, just south of Hobart, where female convicts were kept. It is a World Heritage-listed site now. When I went to Tasmania in 1973 that had not happened. The site would have been desolate and derelict. As it is, most of the buildings are gone and just the skeletons of the buildings are laid out on the ground using lines of gravel. Most of the surrounding wall is intact – stone and brick walls that are thirteen feet high.

As a convict, Sarah spent time here in between assignments to private employers. The women also did contract work here, washing clothes and sewing, hence the name 'factory'. The government used the money to meet the expenses of the prison. Sarah also had a baby here, not an uncommon event, 'father unknown'. The practice was for the women to look after the baby and breastfeed it for six months, then it was taken away to the Orphan School, and the women were punished with a longer sentence for having had a baby.

Sin and sewing and servitude, filling the role of servant for their betters – that was their lot.

Sometimes, the commissioned work was for the ladies and gentlemen of the fledging society. The matron would say to the convict girls, "Imagine, the gown or frock-coat you are sewing today could be adorning the body of a guest at the Governor's Ball next month." In such places, one has to derive what thrill one can from the circumstances. And in among the harshness, the discipline and the struggle, the dampness and the cold, there could be moments of unheralded peace.

The following story is told at the site.

The *Rajah* ship left England in April 1841 with a load of 180 female convicts, bound for Van Diemen's Land. These voyages were perilous, both for the ships and the occupants, who often died of sickness on the way, on a journey that could take three to five months. The *Rajah* arrived in Hobart in July 1841 with the loss of only one woman. The ship's surgeon commented in his journal that the health of all the women was considerably better than when they had left Woolwich, a remarkable fact in those times.

* * * * *

I wonder what distinguished this voyage that made such a difference to the women? It would seem that it was the fact that they were engaged daily on the voyage in the making of a quilt. The women were each sewing a square to be incorporated into the one quilt when they had all finished. They used pieces of materials and thread from the bag of "useful things" they had each been given before the ship left port.

But it is not the quilt itself that is distinctive; it is the fact that, on a voyage characterised by danger and despair, a group of women met daily to sew, to calm their minds in the presence of each other and make something they wanted to be beautiful, every day. That was where the life was, that was the thread that kept them alive.

It would have been of no use for them to rage against their circumstances. It may have been admirable for a short while, but then futility should kick in and make them rethink the wisdom of their rage. Defiance is sometimes all we have, but it may not be the thing that gets us to a fortunate end. The daily patient industry of

2

working on a creation, small though it may be, proved to be the thing that served their survival.

The quilt was made up of all their pieces; they were part of it, and their small personal story and vision was taken up into a larger statement, and despite all the different pieces, due to the differing skills and materials the women used, it was one large, coherent piece – in the end, one. That was the way to step off a ship at the end of the world, knowing that yours was a place in that weave.

The story is commemorated at the Cascades Female Factory site by a sculpture. The quilt that the ladies made has been rendered in coloured metal squares threaded together and raised in a steel frame in one of the yards.

* * * * *

A quilt is a creation that is made up of pieces. It is only at the end that it comes together. I have come to think that our lives are like that. There is none of the planned unfolding that we tend to think of. Our lives are made up of pieces, and many of those pieces may be quite different to each other, and it is often hard to see the connections between one thing and the next. Perhaps a life is complete when all the pieces that need to be made have been made, and at the last, the pieces are composed and sewn together.

Then again, perhaps that is not a universal truth. There are some people's lives that seem to be altogether planned. They start in the top left-hand corner and go the next square and then the next. A committee obviously sat and decided at the beginning how it should be, and the quilt of their life can be read like a page of writing, from word to word and from line to line.

That is not how my life has been. I once got a job as the manager of an organisation, having never done this before, and I did that job for six years. I learned competence. But I never planned to be a manager for life. I was not on the bottom rung of a career ladder. I just felt that I needed to learn how to be a manager. I needed to learn that role and those skills. In my life, that was a small square. I am still not sure how it fits into the quilt that will be my life, at the end.

* * * * *

3

I am talking about quilts because it makes sense of what has been happening. I have left work and my life has changed. It is made up of different things now, and there are always people who will tell you what they think it should be made up of. But this is a new square, and I can fend off the occasional advice and expectations. This square is about writing, which has always been an aspect of my life, but now it is in the foreground. And I am taking my guidance from other occupations (or vocations, or pastimes) – artists and musicians. And what I am hearing is about the process, not so much the product.

An artist I know says that painting is about being quiet, and painting from out of that quietness. A musician I heard talking about his music said that writing a song was not about having a formula – a set structure, a time frame and a visualised audience. No, he said, it was a beginning and an end, but a big space in the middle, and this was the place where you explored a feeling.

When you think about it, this is shocking. The experts say that the plot is the thing, and the characters feed into the plot and something happens that is clever, or terrible, or uplifting, because of the plot. But the musician and the artist are saying that the plot will be evident afterwards. And then there are the ladies, making their small story each day, knowing it will be taken up into a larger story that embodies all of their fellow passengers/prisoners, sitting out on the deck of the ship on good days, sitting inside the cabin on bad days when the ship is rolling violently from side to side, and pitching backwards and forwards with the waves.

I am reminded that 'plot' does not only stand for the steps in a story. It also stands for a plot of land. This is a great thing, because a plot of land is a bit like a quilt. When I was in Tasmania (this time) I went to an old farm, one that went back to the 1820s. It had grown in stages, so that, set out around a centre there were buildings – the main house, the workers' dwellings, the grain store, the shearing shed, the cook house, the blacksmith's shop, and so on. All on a plot of land, and each building was part of the whole, all necessary, all taking their place in the whole, like squares in a quilt. In the end, there is a plot.

* * * * *

4

The ladies of the *Rajah* each had their voice, and it was heard in each square of the quilt they made, a small offering that was accepted, so that afterwards, after it had been put together, it spoke like a choir. The quilt was completed by the end of that long sea voyage, and it was accompanied by a statement from the ladies. The key sentiment in the statement was gratitude, for having survived, and for having spent time in a peace that many of them may never have known. I think it soaked in.

When people looked at the quilt, then, what did they see? The struggles, the desires and the pain of the women? Despair? I am sure it was all there, but I think also, the simple persistence of stitch upon stitch, the fruition of small designs. In other words, what my friend painter talked about, the quietness from which his painting comes. Do you see it? Do you see?

* * * * *

I am travelling through Tasmania. Yesterday I saw another quilt, at the museum in a small town. It was created as a memorial to 150 years of settlement. There were squares representing different aspects of the town, and various significant events, milestones of time in 150 years. It was a public monument, so it celebrated the public face of things, and therefore the quilt was planned systematically, and the women were assigned their part in the tale beforehand. The facts were assembled and dissected, and the appropriate stance was determined towards the facts. I wonder if there were discussions about that. I wonder if there were questions. They were bound to want a quilt that projected a proud, unified view.

I know that the quilt was finished, because it was on display. I don't know about the conversations that were held, or the residual feelings of the women. The past is not an easy thing, not in our society, because we have uprooted everything and paved over it. If I were aboriginal, the quilt would be about the seasons and the weather, and the movements of birds and animals. It would be about what to do in days to come, and how to dance our gratitude for the bounty of the earth. Or we might draw it on the ground with powdered coloured chalk like a group of Tibetan monks, and when we had all seen it and the ceremony had ended, we would brush the

5

chalk back into the mystery, and accept the essential incomprehensibility and wonder of it all.

* * * * *

I travelled to another country town. It was a pleasant journey. When I stopped the car, looking for a place to have morning tea, I was attracted to two wind-blowing signs anchored in the lawn beside a church. One said 'Café' and the other said 'Quilts'. I decided that this was where I would have morning tea. The building was in the grounds of the church, a staid, comforting stone church from the early days of the colony in Tasmania, the days when it was called Van Diemen's Land and the jokes were about demons.

The café had, as one might expect, quilts hung around the walls, but the body of the room was filled with shelves of materials. It was a place where you could choose from a huge array of patterned and coloured materials that would constitute the pieces of your quilt. The café was at one end of the room. It was attended by three women, old and young. Inside the café, the world outside is not to be seen. It is gone, and you are surrounded only by the completed quilts, the results of other women's ideas and diligence, and the possibilities offered by the assortment of materials on offer.

Women talked. There were a couple of men, but they were quiet, content not to lead the conversation in this place. They would go home and mend the mower, or paint a gate. This was a place where women conferred, perhaps discussing the situation of their daughter and son-in-law, and how they were handling their recent separation. "Don't tell me what to do," the son-in-law had said, "I'm not going to change."

I finished my coffee and the slice of carrot and walnut cake, and went back outside. A lady on an outside table with her dog at foot smiled at me. Was that approval for visiting the quilt café? Another piece of the story.

I had forgone a market in Hobart to come to this town today. I had been to that market once, but I had liked it and wanted to go there again. But now, as I walked up towards the town, I saw that there was a market on here today. It was okay that I didn't attend the other one. Now I walked up through the stalls, with their offerings of food and crafts, and craft-made spirits, and heard the music of a violin that was so sweet I felt tears coming. Looking up I could see the hills that surrounded the town, still clothed in trees. The player was a Chinese man dressed in formal wear, white shirt and a long black frock coat.

I stopped at a stall and a woman was saying, "If I ever win the lottery, I am going to hold a beautiful dinner, and I will hire that man to play for the evening." I said I thought that was a lovely idea. She said that she had once bought a CD from a man playing in public like this, and when she got home and played it, the music quality was really poor and she was disappointed.

But I had a contrary story. I had heard a man playing lovely music on the street in Chinatown in Sydney, and I had bought his CD and given it to my mother. She loved it so much that it was the music she ended up playing the most. I saw that the lady was pondering. I wondered if she was disturbed by a story that was different to her own experience, but it seemed that she was contemplating that the experience she had had was not the only possible one. That was my intention.

I was still standing at the stall. It was because the lady tending the stall had called out to me. She didn't know my name but she said, "I know you." I remembered her face, but she filled in the gaps for me. "You were on the same tour the other day. We were in the same group listening to what the guide was saying about the historical house." And so we had. Right up the other end of the island. And now she was selling sweet things at a stall here in this town. I bought some sweets, and we talked. The pieces are connected.

* * * * *

At the beginning of a quilt, there are deliberations. The quilt must be about something, unless you purchase a pattern kit, which you could indeed do at the church café. But they had on display several quilts that were stories. They were what someone wanted to say. They were not a pattern out of a kit. I understand kits. Sometimes making a quilt is about the sewing, that is all. It is like the ladies on the *Rajah*, faced with high seas and uncertainty, and no means of escape. I am sure they pricked their fingers many times with their needles as the waves surged around the ship, but the surgeon said at the end of the journey that he was amazed at the

7

health and disposition of the women, so blooming, so much improved. One might have expected the opposite.

But ordinarily, there are deliberations. If I think of this as life, it is a difficult proposition. For a start, you have one plan at the start, but after a while you see it has already diverted, and you know not where it is headed anymore. As a quilt, is it already a failure? I ask my friend Lilian, who is a quilter, how it works. She laughs and tells me, "There are two answers. The first answer is, you make many quilts. They are small in ambition, and they are just exercises; they are not the master quilt. But you may have one stashed away in a trunk, a blank piece, for the one you know you will do later, when you are ready. I have known women who have done this. I have also known old women who have not started on it."

"Failure?" I asked, tentatively.

"No," she said, emphatically.

I did not press her further on this point, but I asked, "How does one approach an exercise?"

"Ah," she said, "if I am unsure, I start around the outside. I circle it. Sooner or later I will head to the centre. In fact, it's just like a labyrinth, you circle back and forth, long runs, short runs, around and around, always eyeing the centre and thinking, 'I am headed there if I keep doing my steps and thinking.' That's how I do it."

"When you start, how do you start? Do you deliberate?"

Lilian said, "I am circling the question. I started with a pattern that I liked, and I was going to repeat it all the way around the outside, and then the squares started to change, and it was more like the phases of the moon, so I think that's what it will be. Around the outside, there will be a pattern like the phases of the moon. Then we shall see."

"I talked to a painter," I said. "He told me that he starts with an idea of an image, and then he tries to keep his mind still while he is painting it."

"Maybe," said Lilian. "Sometimes. Perhaps."

"Ah," I replied. "Then I talked to a singer who writes songs, and she wanted to write a novel instead, because she said a song is too small – it is just one snapshot, and she wanted a whole plot."

8

"But then there are Bob Dylan's ballads, or Arlo Guthrie's 20-minute saga of Alice's Restaurant. They are songs and they are also stories."

"You could argue that," I said, "but I see the point she was making."

"So, is a quilt a song or a novel?" Lilian smiled.

"How many squares does it have?" I replied.

"There is that," she said. "How many squares will there be in yours?"

"I am thinking thirty-two, that's eight by four. Or maybe forty-eight. After all, in the end, one wants to stay warm at night."

"A person might start with four squares," she said. "But you could be aiming for ten by eight, that's eighty squares. To do that, you are probably thinking of patterns and repetition."

I asked, "Would that be a snapshot, once again, or could it be a story?"

"A snapshot, as you say, could be a good thing. Like a mantra, it is the effect it has on the mind of the creator. In the China of ancient days, they called it fixing the omen, which is to make an image into something permanent."

"I want to make a quilt with words," I said. "I want to fix the omen that way."

"You mean you want to sew a quilt where each square is made up of words? You could do that. Other people have done it. Sure."

"No, I don't think that's it. I want to make a quilt that is made up of pieces, where each piece is a story, and it is all sewn together somehow. And it all fits to make a bigger story."

Lilian looked at me opaquely. "I'm having trouble translating," she said.

"So am I," I replied.

"What do you want it to say?"

"First of all, I have to choose some pieces."

"Well, don't make the mistake of thinking that that is difficult. Now that you've said that, just get on with it."

9

Sewing a square

I travelled to a town where there used to be an asylum. Now the asylum is shut down completely, but there are two lengths left of the brick wall which used to enclose it. The walls extend over one hundred metres each way, four metres high. It was originally a hospital that started in the 1830s. It was later that it became an asylum for the insane. Given the treatment of convicts, the circumstances from which they came, and the circumstances many of them endured on an ongoing basis, it is not surprising that madness occurred. It was said that they had become afflicted with the worst of maladies, loss of reason.

The institution endured until the late twentieth century, housing people who were deemed to have mental illness or an intellectual disability. Eventually, a government inquiry led to its closure. The stories that were revealed had just been too awful. It was not even demolished tidily to extinguish the stain; most of the buildings were simply abandoned, and have become populated by a variety of causes and eccentric businesses. The Lions Club and the Masonic Lodge have accommodations in the yard, and there is a café.

As if to indicate the nature of the events that happened within the four walls, one building is still standing, but it is smashed. All the windows have been smashed, and doors have been removed. A giant hole gapes in one side of the building, as if it were hit with a wrecking ball, but why is there just the one hole? It speaks like anger unleashed.

The sights within the grounds are even more dramatic. The place has become an abandoning ground for old vehicles, dozens of them, carcases rusting away in untidy lines, on the asphalt and parked in the grass. None of them is restored; they are rotting away, and tyres, wheels and windows are missing. It seems as if violence has been used on many of them. There are cars, buses, tractors, cranes, Land Rovers and trucks. Nothing will ever become of any of them. It is as if people wanted to put all the rotten things in these grounds, to house them like demons and put them at a distance from ordinary life, so that ordinary life might go on.

Did they mean this as a reference to the people who were inmates here, the hapless crazy ones, or to the systems and practices that were in vogue, the harshness, the violence and the abuse that came to light in the inquiry? I think the derelict vehicles depict a blanket revulsion of everything that happened here, and of wanting to put every dark thing away here, so that the rest of life might be alright. There is a combie van, pale blue and white, with the front end shot full of bullet holes. The back wheels are gone so it sits up at an unnatural angle, like those kangaroos you see by the side of the road after they've been hit by a car: body stiff, one leg up in the air.

There is one bus which says it was the original tour bus for AC/DC in 1973, and that may be true. I have not seen many buses making that claim. And there is a gravestone for sale, lying against the side of a truck between two gates of rusting metal. It has been used by John Webb, who died in 1871 aged 45 years, and his wife, Matilda, who died in 1864 aged 39 years, and two of their children who died in infancy. There was no price on it but it is available.

There are businesses here occupying the old buildings. A few of them are styled as antique stores, and they are indeed crammed with old items, room upon room of them. It is like a museum of the twentieth century, right from its beginning. There are machines, clothes, crockery, furniture. It is bewildering and overwhelming. I can't imagine anyone buying any of these things. It is just on display like a vast collection of once-loved or once-useful relics.

I overheard a conversation. The lady at the desk was talking to some visitors. This building was not the place where inmates were kept; it had been the male staff quarters. But it clearly had its horrors. She said that one day an older man was outside the shop, but he wouldn't come in. She went outside to talk to him. It happened that he had been a boy kept here, for some reason. And at night there were male staff who violated him in this building. He wept in front of the lady.

So, 'keeping shop' here is not just about bargaining on prices for old wares and collecting the money. The real job is to watch for the wounded and do healing, in what little way one can. The scars run deep. You can sense the shadow. It is in the very earth of the place, in the very bricks of the buildings.

This is a square, then, and yes, it is a snapshot, just that. But when all the squares have been put together and sewn, it will be a quilt, and there may be a plot to it. I ask Lilian about this, and she says yes, it is a snapshot, and she can see how it could be a square. She asks me, "What comes next?"

I say, "The thing about squares is that they can be quite different."

"Then you will have to see how they fit together, when you have made them."

Another square

A quilt can be made up of many squares, but how are the squares related to each other? Is it merely a visual relationship – the squares make a pattern that is pleasing and balanced? It could be. My mother made a couple of quilts like that – not with materials, but with crocheted squares in coloured patterns.

I talk to Lilian again. She says this to me: "A patchwork can be metaphor for there being no pattern at all. It is a way of saying there is no progress, the squares just fall together. It is random, and that's a metaphor for life."

"When I have finished my stories, will they be anything more than patchwork, then?" I ask. Lilian doesn't always answer.

* * * * *

Travelling down the east coast of Tasmania, I stopped at a small town on the verge of a large bay, and found that it boasted a historical museum. The building was old, and it had originally been a school. This area had been settled very early on in the colonial history of Van Diemen's Land. It was a farming and timber area. I had expected to find old farming tools and the accoutrements of simple country living in the colonial days. Instead, I came upon an exhibition of paintings of native plants and flowers.

At first I assumed that the exhibition was visiting, that it was a rural offering from the greater resources of Hobart, but although that was true, that would have misrepresented it. The paintings on display were actually prints of the originals, and they did indeed come from the state library in Hobart, but only because the originals were too fragile to travel. The originals had been painted by a lady who lived in this part of the world in the 1800s: Louisa Ann Meredith.

The paintings were beautiful. She had painted many native plants and flowers, and butterflies too. The colours were vivid, and the shapes seemed true. It reminded me, by contrast, of many of the early drawings and paintings that had been done of Australian plants, birds and animals. To our eye they seem distorted, as if the original artists regarded what they found as so strange that they could not represent it accurately. Their kangaroos and kookaburras are stretched in the wrong places, and awkward; their drawings of Aborigines look as if they were trying to fit them into some model that was more familiar to them.

This is what struck me as extraordinary about Louisa Meredith's paintings. There seemed to be none of these distortions going on; she was seeing all of these plants, which must have been unfamiliar to her (she was born in Birmingham and grew up there), with utter truth, no preconceptions or biases interfering with her eye. How could this be so? I read that she grew up at the time when people in British cities were agitating for electoral reform, and she learned to think independently and express herself fearlessly on religious and social issues. I think a mind like that has a truer eye, to see what is simply there rather than resorting back to some convention and making it conform to that.

The notes in the exhibition said that she took great care to represent the colours of the leaves and flowers (and the butterflies) accurately. She did many experiments to find the right ingredients to make the right colours, and her work has been praised for that.

All of Louisa's work happened in parallel with her husband's life. Charles was at various times a land-holder with flocks of sheep, a police magistrate, and a member of the colonial parliament, as well as being Treasurer for a period of time. Louisa continued to paint, and also to write. Her first literary works had been published before her marriage, in England – newspaper articles supporting the views of the Chartists. Her first book was published when she was twenty-three – a collection of poems which included her own illustrations.

Her first book from Australia was published (in London) five years after her arrival, giving her frank but astute comments about life in the New South Wales colony, but by now Louisa, Charles and a young son were living in Van Diemen's Land, and she was painting the wildlife that she found there. She produced hundreds of paintings over her long life. Her wildflower drawings won medals in the Melbourne Exhibition of 1866. Some of her illustrations were presented in a book called *Tasmanian Friends and Foes, Feathered, Furred and Finned: A Family Chronicle of Country Life*, published in 1880.

Louisa studied the plants, insects, seaweeds and fish of Tasmania's east coast, and she was an active member of the Society for the Prevention of Cruelty to Animals. In Parliament, her husband was active in preserving native flora and fauna, and he introduced a bill to protect the black swan from extinction.

Apart from her wildlife illustrations, Louisa also produced seven books of poems between 1842 and 1891. The Tasmanian government granted her a pension of £100 in 1884 for 'distinguished literary and artistic services' to the colony. Her husband had died in 1880.

In her late seventies, and despite constant pain from sciatica, Louisa even travelled to London to oversee the publication process for her last book, *Bush Friends in Tasmania: Last Series*. She died in Victoria in 1895.

* * * * *

I showed this story to Lilian. "It's very different to the previous square," she commented.

"It is a different kind of square, I admit," I replied. "It's what turned up next. And it's also true."

"Can you make it fit in the same quilt?" she asked.

"Are you suggesting it's just random, a patchwork, as they say?"

"No, I'm suggesting there could be a great battle going on here, and who will win?"

"It's too early, the squares are still gathering," I replied, "but I can tell you one other thing about Louisa."

"What's that?"

"She was a good dressmaker. She sewed all the family's clothes."

"Ah, then."

"And another thing."

"What's that?"

"At the same museum, the lady at the desk told me I should go into the front room. When I looked at her quizzically, she said, 'All the war things are in there.' And she added, 'Even if you're not interested in the war things, you should see the billiard table.' And as if to answer my unsaid question, she added, 'It's no ordinary billiard table. This one is ten percent larger than normal, and it's made out of Tasmanian blackwood, with an Italian marble base for the table. It weighs around five tons.'"

"Did you go to see the table?"

"I did. It dominated the room. It seemed enormous, and it was so finely made, all that polished dark wood surrounding the expanse of the table. The lady on the desk also told me that the idea of the billiard table was that the soldiers returning from the war could take their minds off the unspoken horrors of the war by playing billiards. There was an air of scepticism in her voice."

"I imagine so," said Lilian. "It was more likely to have encouraged drinking. And you can't play billiards forever. You have to find a way back to living; you have to find a new life. Do you think, when the men were gathered around the table, following the smooth movement of a round coloured ball on that smooth green surface, almost silent, that the subject of their wartime experiences ever came up?"

"I imagine it did. It could have shown in a slight tremor, or a momentary hesitation before someone went to take the cue to plan his next shot. And then the game would go on."

We pondered.

"They had a collection of birds' eggs there as well," I added.

"Where, at the museum?"

15

"Yes, in the old schoolroom. There were big ones, like ducks' eggs, and tiny ones, like wrens' eggs. All in little nests of their own. Some of them were so small, it is hard to imagine what a newly hatched baby chick would look like."

"Things of wonder," smiled Lilian.

"New life," I smiled.

Square 3

Lilian asks me what's next. I am still travelling. This leg of the journey is of a different kind. I have been here once before, in 1973. I think I could be one of only a very few people who have seen Tasmania before, but not seen it again in forty-six years. Is it still the same? Is it different?

I hitch-hiked then. It was not thought to be an unsafe thing to do; perhaps it was not entirely sensible, but it was not unthinkable. It was what I wanted to do. It had been important. I went to towns down the east coast of Tasmania. I was young, twenty-three, and I met other young people on the way. We stopped at youth hostels – I don't know what they call them now; I assume they still exist.

I met some of the same people over the course of a week. We talked, crazy talk, full of opinions and newfound knowledge, full of dreams. What a wonder – full of dreams! I remember Paul, one night at a bar after we had all had several drinks, confiding that he wanted to stay in Tasmania and build a log cabin. That leaves a question: did he ever do it? Is he still here on the island somewhere, living the life of that dream?

I stopped in one of the same towns, booking a room at a motel overnight. It was a perfectly normal motel room except for the large painting on the wall. The painting was of a line of combie vans parked at a beach, all facing away from the water so that, sleeping in the back and with the back door open, you would be looking at the surf, and hearing the noise of it. The combie vans all had white roofs, and with their headlights they looked as if they all had their eyes open. Another combie van was coming towards them like a new friend. A dream, and for a time, real enough.

I walked down the road in the afternoon, to the wharves. It was a fishing town, and a place where a boat would take you out on the bay for the day. There are new facilities about, but it is the same place, the water, the inlets, the land across the bay. There is a houseboat for sale, with a mobile phone number festooned across one side. There is a fish-and-chips restaurant on the docks, obviously well-patronised.

Down the street in the town I turn a corner and there is a shop at the end of the street with a sign. It is not the name of the shop, or is it? It says "Books, Coffee, Wine, Beer". Drawn by the uniqueness of the offering, I head towards it. It is clear when I enter that it is a bookshop, a second-hand bookshop more than anything else, although, when I get to the end of the aisles I look to the left and see a nook that is a creditable coffee shop, and when I look at the counter, it has the makings of a bar.

All the chairs and tables in the coffee shop section are hand-made out of pine. I am not an authority on Huon Pine, but it could have been that. The man behind the bar is old, let's say seventy. He has a trimmed beard, which is grey, and long grey hair in a ponytail. I think he has been here a long time. I think of Paul and 1973, and his log-cabin dream. This man is not Paul. He is an ex-American. I have met a few of them, and have always thought they came here for the right reasons, looking for a peaceful lifestyle.

I order coffee, and I look around. There are around 10,000 books here, spread across a wide variety of subjects. Back near the door there were some recent books on show, but the bulk of these books have been here a long time. And you know he has built this collection himself, and it's a mixture of what he thought would be popular with customers and what he was interested in himself.

I suspect he weighs up book customers on the basis of what they buy. He could be critical of them for wanting a particular book, or reluctant to let a particular book go. He could want to know, badly, why you chose a certain book, because it has some meaning in his own past, and he wants to plumb that depth with them.

More books kept cropping up around me as I drank my coffee, and I had to get up and walk around. There were shelves behind some of the tables, and I noticed an aisle of books over near one wall. I was still trying to absorb the range of topics, everything from fiction to gardening, theatre, history, fishing, books on Asian countries, and a sprinkling of philosophy. I was trying to make sense of the man.

There was a post in the middle of the room, and I thought of Paul's log cabin again. On the post were news clippings from the local papers, some of them going back to the 1980s. This man and the other people involved in the shop then had been involved in community events for local causes. He had made this town his home, and the community his own.

I left, on my way, bidding farewell to the man. There is a certain point, maybe when you are around forty, when you reflect on the dream. Did it come true? Is it true – are you in it now? Or do the circumstances you have created fall short? Or can you settle for this? Is it okay, and the important thing is that you learn to love it? Are adolescent dreams unfulfillable anyway? Is that their nature?

Many times, this period of reflection is complicated by the fact that there are two people in a relationship doing this, sometimes separately, sometimes together. And if the relationship fails at this point, that can precipitate another crisis. I didn't know anything about the man from "Books, Coffee, Wine, Beer", but at this point in life, he seems like a nice man with some measure of peace and an active intelligence.

It was when I got back to the motel that I realised I did not have my glasses. This is an inconvenience, because reading is difficult without them, and I am a long way from home, where my spare pair is located. I figured I must have left them in the café, because the rest of the time I was walking. I decided to go straight back to the café, because it was getting late in the afternoon, and it was a twenty-minute walk.

When I got there, the door was already shut and the lights were out. I guess not many books are sold after 4:30 pm. That meant I had to go without my glasses overnight, and come back in the morning and hope the glasses were here.

The man at the motel was cheerful. He was outside building something out of wood to enhance the facilities at the motel. He said not to worry, "Everyone is honest around here. You'll get your glasses back in the morning." And of course it was alright. When I returned in the morning, the shop was open, lights on again, and the man was there.

He said, "You're the guy, aren't you? From yesterday? I saw your glasses on the table only a few minutes after you'd left, and I ran down the street after you. But you had already gone. You must walk like the wind."

I laughed. I had not been walking quickly. Clearly, I had been walking on Sydney time, and he had been running on Tasmanian time. I thanked him, and it looked as if I had plenty of time, so I ordered a cup of coffee. There was time enough to get to the next town. And there was. When I got there, the tide in the river was out and everything was perfectly still.

Square 4

I have been here and there in Tasmania, from the west coast to the east coast and up through the middle. I have stories that occurred in the compartment of the old days, and stories that spill into the present.

The west of Tasmania drew rough men in the late 1800s. Mostly they came to find ore and make money that way. An unusual fellow called James 'Philosopher' Smith was a prospector and he had found tin, and that was mined with great profit, so others came to emulate him. Smith was the child of two convicts, and his upbringing had been hard, but somehow he had learned to read, and was a voracious reader across a wide variety of subjects, hence the 'Philosopher' tag. He would pack his swag and go bush for months at a time. It was on one of these trips in the 1870s that he discovered what he thought to be tin ore, and so it proved to be.

A tin mine was established, and the mine attracted others to the region, even though the hills were steep, the terrain was rugged, and the forests were difficult to penetrate. Gold was found as well as tin, so there was the promise of wealth to tempt the hardy. Somehow they made camps in the bush and scratched out a living, and occasionally someone would strike it lucky. An indication of the temper of the times was given by a funeral that was held in 1897 at Corinna, a tiny shanty town on the Pieman River. The publican, Gam Webster, had died.

Over a hundred men from the surrounding hills heard the news and turned up for the funeral. Some of them came from the other side of the river, and dangerously overloaded the small punt that carried people across. Gam Webster was a well-respected and well-liked man. He had a reputation for kindness and generosity, and he had stuck around in the area for many years, and brought his wife with him, so his loss was felt deeply by the locals.

Such feelings found their natural outlet in Gam's tiny hotel, which was no bigger than an average-sized house. Given that the publican was dead, the bar was breached, and by nightfall, drunkenness was almost universal. Noisy brawling went on throughout the night. By the morning, the minister, the Reverend F.G. Copelland, who had arrived to conduct the funeral, had had enough and took the law into his own hands by ordering the bar closed and locking everyone out of the hotel.

It was said that few men were sober for the funeral. Reverend Copelland fulfilled his duty as best he could, and the grave can still be found near the present-day town. One visitor to the area at the time said it was "The roughest place it has been my experience to strike". They were the boom times, and the town had more than thirty buildings, including two hotels, a post office, stores and shops, slaughter yards and residences.

The *Zeehan and Dundas Herald* newspaper published a fine obituary for Mister Gamelial Webster (18th August 1897), who left behind him several brothers and sisters and a wife and six children, who all lived in the area. The obituary concluded, "Beneath his rough exterior there beat the generous heart of the man ever ready to assist his fellow kind, even at a loss to himself, and the many who have known and partaken of his hospitality will join with us in conveying a genuine expression of condolence to his sorrowing widow and family."

The equivalent of the hotel these days is a building that houses a bar, a restaurant and a small alcove selling souvenirs. Fishermen and walkers stop in here to eat, have a drink and swap stories. There is still a punt that can take you across the river, and there are cabins nearby where you can stay overnight in comfort. There is electricity. The road is still gravel, although one imagines it is in a better state than when folk came to town for Gam's funeral.

I think that, like James 'Philosopher' Smith and Gam Webster, many of the folk who lived in this place were not really hoping to 'strike it rich'. I think they had found a place where they liked to be, for all its roughness and the hardships it could throw your way. I think it is truer to say that many of them eked out a living. The fact that now and then someone would find a good lode of tin or a ridiculously big nugget of gold just kept the outward rationale for living there alive.

For many of them, the truth was, it was a haven, it was a manageable wilderness where solace was found. I suspect that these were people who had never found such solace elsewhere, in cities or towns or in engines of mass industry. Theirs was the modest, almost laughable machine that generated more noise than effect, and was not working more often than it worked. The old tracks around here exhibit sufficient examples of rusty configurations of buckets and cog wheels and levers to be testimony to that.

I saw an old photo of two men holding up a string of fish on a pole, all of the fish weighing probably two kilograms each. Nowadays we would decry such a catch as excessive and dangerous to the ongoing fish population, but then it was not like that. There were only a few men, relative to the wilderness, and the wilderness was a place of plenty. They were living in the midst of bounty, but also knowing there were times when they would eat well, and other times when they wouldn't. Nowadays we have grown enormously in number and we have reached our limit, and our machines magnify our effect, and whatever we do exhausts the earth. We have fish farms and everything is (necessarily) controlled. We are never afraid that we will not eat. We are comfortable, but at great cost.

In the present-day Tasmania, I found another haven, another hotel, billed as being beside a lake. But the lake was not a natural lake; there was a straight mound of earth across the valley – it was the work of humans and machines. Accordingly, the water had dozens of dead trees standing in it, dead skeletons with their crowns broken off, congregating in the shallows like aimless, dejected phantoms. Ahead, the water stretched out like a main road for speed boats.

Having to look through the dead trees, I found it difficult to imagine life beneath that surface. I was told cheerfully that there were fish, and that the department made sure there were always fish by restocking it every year. I was at the end of a dirt road, well, a dirt road that only ran a few hundred more metres. The road gave access to about fifty rough shacks along the shore of the lake.

A sign at the start of the shacks pronounced the lake to be a storage reservoir. It had a map of the lake with the water painted blue, and the names that had been given to all the little bays around the shore. The map was to the scale of eight chains to the inch and measurements were given in gallons and feet, so the sign had to date from before the mid-1960s, when Australian money and measurements began to be converted to metric. The dam had been built in 1883 at a cost of 12,500 pounds. Its area was 1,500 acres and its average depth was fourteen and three-quarters feet.

The sign was a welcome to visitors from what I assume was the local branch of the Northern Tasmanian Fishing Association (NTFA) and the more transparently named Shack Owners Club. The shacks were clearly not laid out on the basis of surveyed lines; it looked more like tents laid out at a camping site, or even more like tents laid out at a music festival. So how could you own a shack here? I found out that you could purchase a licence from the local council to build a shack, and there was a limit to how many days a year you could live in your shack. It was intended to cater for fishermen who wanted to stay here by the lake.

The hotel where I stayed was called an inn. It had been built in the 1880s, so, around the same time that the dam was built. It was more an assemblage of related structures than a building. There was the bar, which led into a large restaurant area and onto a games room with a pool table and a darts board. Out the back through a dark corridor there were rooms, and that slipped out into a courtyard that seemed to have been under-appreciated for quite a few years.

In the bar were about half a dozen people. It would have taken twice as many to fill an egg carton. I am including the pub owner and at least one staff; it was a little hard to tell, because if someone wanted a drink and the publican wasn't there, they just went behind the bar, poured a drink and put some money in the till. It was late afternoon, and the crew in the bar seemed to have been in the bar for some hours, drinking slowly.

The talk was of day-to-day stuff, what Bill had been doing, and how that table was definitely going to get fixed the day after tomorrow; it was organised. Someone went out and got into their dune buggy, yes, not a car, but a dune buggy, to go back to their shack to get a packet of Girl Guides biscuits that someone else in the bar had promised to buy. After that there was talk about money and change, and who hadn't bought biscuits yet.

What put it all into perspective was a photo hanging above the bar. It was the publican and his wife getting married, circa early 1970s, a black-and-white print in a frame. I checked the face of the publican and one of the women at the bar, and yes, it was them, the same couple. Hanging up in the other corner was a colour television with the daily news playing, with this quirk – the sound was turned off and what we could hear coming from the speakers was a country singer playing his country album. I liked it; it put the banality of the news at a distance and brought the music into the foreground.

Academically, it could be said that this ploy was a clever way of recontextualising the relevance of the daily news. Here was a community living over an hour from town, and even then it was a small town, living their daily lives in a somewhat self-sufficient way. They lived near a lake, and they probably enjoyed a regular meal of freshly caught fish. When it was freezing cold in winter, they would huddle around the open fire in the bar and keep warm, and talk. You could say it was a haven.

There was a choice of rooms; there weren't too many people using the accommodation the night I was there. The publican asked me if I wanted a single or double bed. I said 'double'. He sighed and said, "Well, that's fine, but that room's next to where the cook sleeps, and he snores. This place was built in 1885 and the walls aren't exactly thick."

Nevertheless, I chose the double bed. Perhaps the cook's snoring wouldn't be so bad. It was a long rectangular room lined with timber panelling. It didn't seem so bad, and the roof was ten feet high. I like high ceilings. It wasn't a big room, but it would serve the purpose. The view outside the window was onto a paddock with some kind of derelict machine standing patiently in it, waiting for the next crop to harvest, or the next mining venture; I couldn't tell. I can identify rust.

Later on I ordered dinner. I was told the cook started work at 5:30 pm. I ordered something that seemed safe, and was pleasantly surprised that it was well-cooked – a large serving, of course, but not burnt, dry, drowning in gravy or tasteless. As the evening went on, the cook probably cooked ten meals altogether. I saw him when he finished work. He entered the bar and took his cook's cap off. He was in his fifties, a quiet man. He went behind the bar and poured himself a beer, then sat down at the bar, opened a crossword book and started doing a crossword.

Other people were still talking. Some of the personnel had changed, but not a lot. I noticed a printed sign above the bar that said "No shots until after 8 PM." Just after 8 pm, the son of one of the women in the bar walked in. He was probably just eighteen. The mother walked behind the bar, got out two glasses for shots, filled them, and gave one to her son. The son skulled it down. This ritual only happened the once; there was no repetition.

Another woman brought in her son, who was much younger, about twelve. She asked the publican if her son could have one game of darts in the games room. The publican said there was no one using the room at the moment, so that would be okay. The mother said, yes, it would only be one game, because then her son had to go to bed.

I didn't hear the cook snore during the night, just a little bit around dawn, and it wasn't even too loud. I suppose he has a few shifts over the course of the week, and he sleeps over after his shifts before heading back to town.

I left early and the dirt road was deserted. The bush was quiet. I saw one small pademelon, which crossed the road in front of me, unperturbed by my presence, and perceiving no threat.

* * * * *

"Two stories," said Lilian.

24

"About havens," I said. "I think most people don't want to change the world, or perform on a big stage. They want steadiness and refuge. They want a place they can trust as a haven."

"There's a quilt in that," she replied, "although probably set out in a more regular manner than the shacks you described. Perhaps that's what's comforting about quilts – the steady regularity of them, square beside square beside square."

"So far, my squares are unstitched," I replied. "I am just accumulating them. That's okay, isn't it?"

"The ladies of the *Rajah* just sewed their squares day by day," smiled Lilian. "The sea rocked and the waves tumbled. In the end, if nothing else, there will be a quilt, and the quilt will keep someone warm."

Square 5

One of the reasons I came to Tasmania was to look for signs of Sarah Crosby, my great great grandmother, my father's mother's mother's mother. No, I am not looking for ghosts, just some sense of where she had been. She was Irish, born in the County of Waterford between 1830 and 1833, the daughter of a farming family. If you count the years, knowing that the Great Potato Famine occurred between 1845 and 1849, you see that she was somewhere between twelve and fifteen years old when that all started. She leaves Ireland – why and how? – and works for a while as a servant in the city of Bath, England. But she ends up in London, homeless.

On a cold winter's night in January 1849, hungry and alone, she stands in a line outside the Refuge for the Houseless Poor, a charity-run refuge for the many people who were not winners in the industrial revolution, those without work or any means to keep a roof over their heads. For some reason that is not stated at her subsequent trial or in the newspaper reports, Constable John Smith tells her to move on, she will not get a bed here tonight. There is shouting and swearing. Sarah is seized with desperation. She grabs a penknife out of her bag and stabs him in the arm, repeatedly. Constable Smith and a Sergeant wrestle her roughly to the ground. She bites one of them, and her left cheek is slashed in the struggle.

In the end, she does get a bed for the night, in prison. When she comes up for trial, the judge is not impressed. Not only has Sarah attacked a policeman in the course of his duties, she is Irish and ungrateful to the English who have done so much for them. He deems that she will be a "fit and useful subject for the colonies" and sentences her to transportation for seven years. Strangely, when the newspapers report on the trial, they do not highlight the barbarity of the Irish; they see her desperation – a young, tiny girl alone, a starving stranger in a cold city.

Sarah spent almost a year in London prisons before she was shipped out to Van Diemen's Land. I'm sure she had heard the stories. It was a bad year for prisons in London – typhoid had broken out in one prison, in the crowded, cold, damp, stone cells, so badly that the authorities had to move all the women to another prison. It was December 1849 when Sarah boarded the *St Vincent* for Hobart Town, along with 205 other female convicts.

They were some of the last convicts ever sent to Australia. Times had been changing, and by 1853, most transportation had stopped. The colonies had started to burst out of their identity as a prison at a comforting distance from the glory of the empire. Ironically, the colonies wanted to be part of the empire. Over the following fifty years, it became prudent for ex-convicts to start to hide their own pasts. Sarah's own children certainly knew this.

When female convicts arrived at Hobart, they were initially sent to the Cascades Female Factory, a couple of miles to the south of the city. They were disembarked from the ship before dawn so as not to cause any disturbance to the public, and marched the distance to the prison. Their first sight would have been the stone walls, thirteen feet high and over a hundred yards long, with Mount Wellington towering over the establishment. They would grow accustomed to its long shadow in the cold days of winter.

Sarah and her fellow convicts were considered to be lucky – the Female Factory had been so overcrowded that new quarters had been built a year or so before she arrived. It had been the same problem as in the London prisons: cold, damp, overcrowded conditions, no fresh air and poor food.

Sarah had been sick for most of the voyage to Australia, at one point throwing up about a pint of dark blood. Towards the end of the voyage the doctor considered that she was cured, and perhaps she was; perhaps there is something to be said about sea air.

Sarah's time as a convict was truncated, because in March 1853 she married Edward Lewis, a man who had finished his time as a convict and was then serving as a special constable, a not uncommon transition. If a convict married, they were released and came under the supervision of their spouse until the expiration of their sentence.

Sarah had been assigned to households on several occasions, but she had also been sent back to the prison. She may have misbehaved, or been deemed to be lazy or insolent. And then, about a year after her arrival in Hobart Town, she had become pregnant. Had she found some temporary comfort amid the terrors of this far-flung land, or had a man forced himself on her? That sometimes occurred, and sometimes it was the master of the house where they worked who was the culprit. Sometimes women would misbehave solely to get expelled from the house. The Female Factory could be safer.

I found the entry for the birth of the baby in the government's registry of births: Mary Ann Crosby, born 27th April 1851, father unknown. I haven't found out what happened to Mary Ann Crosby. The most likely thing was that she was nursed at Sarah's breast for six months, then taken away and put in the Orphans' School and brought up to learn useful skills to be a servant. Many children died. On the hillside behind the site of the Cascades Female Factory, a place of children's burials is known. There is a block of flats on the site now.

Most of the stone and brick walls are still standing for three of the five yards that used to exist. Inside, none of the original buildings is standing. Their outlines have been marked with rows of basalt gravel. It is like walking on a life-size plan, crunching across gravel and marking out the basalt lines of the outlines of the buildings. It was a sunny day when I went; one had to try to imagine the dark insides of the buildings the women had occupied.

At various places around the yards there are sculptures – steel renditions of furniture such as chairs, tables, beds, washing tubs and babies' cots. They have been left unpainted, so they all have the beautiful reddish patina of rust and you are reminded of time. There was a clothes line with washing on it, emblematic of the contract washing that the women did for outside clients. Along one small wall, the first names of women are inscribed in the steel, in alphabetical order. I followed the alphabet and found 'Sarah'.

I went on a tour and the guide was well-informed. I shared some information about Sarah Crosby with the tour group. The yard to which Sarah would have gone, in 1850, was the one that had just been built, and it was also the yard where women with babies were kept. It was lighter, airier, and the new place was not riddled with fleas. The women would wash or sew during the day. The guide told us the story about the matron (yes, that was her title) encouraging the women with the thought that the garment they were sewing might be worn by a guest at the Governor's Ball.

There was a strange mix of discipline and reform in the management of the female convicts. In one sense, the women were both a management problem for the government and a resource to be used, both for the good of the government and for the free settlers. On the other hand, they were a moral challenge, and the mission was to save these women from their immoral past so they could live as upright maids and wives. The experience of convict women like Sarah must have been sometimes confusing, with times of rage and want woven together inextricably with moments of calm, just like the women on the *Rajah*.

The guide described the class system, with only the first-class convicts being eligible for outside work. There was a second class, and a "crime class". Sarah must have been a 'first class' convict for much of her time, because she had several stints working outside for employers. Some of her time was spent at Brickfield Hiring Depot at North Hobart, which was not intended as a prison but merely as accommodation for women who were waiting for a position with a private employer. It appears that they earned some money for their work.

The guide showed some work that had been done by convict women. It was as fine as needlework might be done by women anywhere who have skill and time and aptitude, and it required an effort of imagination to consider how the women daily crossed the gulf between the fineness of their detailed work, and its cleanliness, and their living quarters that must have been filthy and rough.

I wonder if Sarah had been a seamstress and had sat with the other women working quietly on fine garments or functional daily clothes. All I know is that she probably grew up on a farm, she didn't know how to read or write, and she had served time as a servant in Bath, England. Perhaps she even learned how to sew during her time as a convict. That would have been good – after she married Edward Lewis she had four daughters and a son.

I walked back to Hobart, given that multitudes of women had walked the other way before me, in far less congenial circumstances. On my way to my hotel I passed the Anglican Cathedral, St David's, and the bells were pealing. I noticed, because it was not the automatic pealing of a regular refrain, but the work of human hands. There were people in the tower, doing whatever it was you have to do to make bells ring, at precisely the right times to make the music.

I sat and listened to it for ten minutes. The notes echoed across the streets. One can have thoughts and opinions about churches and religions, and the nature of reality and society, and sometimes one can simply sit and listen to bells. When it ended, I walked around the corner past the church door, and I saw a sign: "Bellringers wanted" and a contact number.

* * * * *

What did Lilian think?

"The quilt is getting bigger," she said. And she also said, "Perhaps Sarah sewed the squares for a quilt."

"What would the quilt have been for?" I asked.

"I think you know that," she smiled.

"Ah, yes, to remember Ireland."

Square 6

I went to Salamanca markets in Hobart, on a Saturday morning. Many of my friends told me I had to do this if I went to Tasmania, so it seemed compulsory. But I am partial to markets anyway. I think it is about being in a communal space where cars have been banished, and where the lines and rules have not been defined by big industry. The weather was fine, sunshine with a chance of showers, and a cool breeze blowing but not too hard.

I started at the top and walked down through the aisle of tents. I was amongst hundreds of stalls, and many hundreds of people. I have happy memories of markets from when I lived in the country, and from music festivals. It's good to remember, when your mind has been ground down to functional matters in daily experience, that there is feeling, beauty and hopefulness, and there are people who are honouring that, probably more than you are. But it's okay.

I was not looking to acquire. I am travelling, and I don't wish to add to the weight of my luggage. And it is a good discipline to look without acquiring. You can appreciate and be inspired. And there is always coffee and food! In this way I was making my way down the aisle of stalls. There were catches of music, there were people talking, and there was sunshine deciding to be persistent.

It was lovely, with many fine things for sale – crafts, food, jewellery, clothes, books and artwork, and many types of alternative lifestyles on show. There were four or five stalls where the author was selling their book, which surprised me. A couple of them were tough-guy adventurer stories, but not all. One was a children's book. Do people buy books at markets? Clearly they do here.

Among all this, I stopped at a stall selling cards and larger artworks – prints. I really liked them; I liked the way the artist looked at things. It was gentle but not weak. There was a certain self-possession about the people she depicted, and a love of nature along with it – sweetness. The stallholder, the artist, was sitting reading a book, and of course I looked at the book. Usually when you do this, the person gets defensive and tries to hide the book. But she didn't; in fact, she seemed delighted.

She started to tell me why it was a good book, instead of turning to talk about her artwork. The book was by G.K. Chesterton: *Orthodoxy*, which is about two generations out of date for most current readers. She handed me the book and invited me to read a passage. The book was first published in 1908, but this was a recent edition, dated 2009. She said she was glad his work was still being published.

She said she liked to read slowly and digest what was being said. She used to slide over descriptive passages, but now she reads those descriptions word by word, and enjoys them. I told her I had watched a Youtube video recently that talked about slow reading, and it gave the same reasons. Speed has intruded into every part of our lives, but it is making us gloss over our moment-by-moment experience.

I loved her pictures. They were contemplative images of young women, one, for example, walking along a beach with a bunch of flowers held in her hands behind her. The petals were trailing off. She said it was about those times when your expectations have not been met, but then you come to see that the ocean washes everything away and you start to move past the sense of loss; you start to find the silver linings.

One of the pieces was different. It wasn't in a contemporary setting; it was a young woman in old-fashioned clothes, with a little girl beside her, on a beach. There was a bay and a sailing ship, with a dark mountain behind it. It gave me a shock. It could have been my Sarah Crosby beneath the shadow of Mount Wellington. I told her it reminded me of my great great grandmother who was an Irish girl who had been sent to Hobart in 1850 on the *St Vincent*. She said she had painted it for those women, the convicts who were still women, still wives and still mothers.

So, I did acquire some things at the market, and they did not add to my load at all.

Square 7

I had been in Hobart a few days, and I knew my way around most of the streets near the centre of the city, and I had found a few decent places to eat, just modest, good food of the Thai, Vietnamese and Indian kind. Late one afternoon I was scouting for a restaurant that I hadn't tried before, but as I was walking down the street, the next corner attracted me, so I walked there.

Then I felt I should turn right and walk that way. It came into my mind as a simple, direct instruction, "Go right here". The thought that was coming to me was that I had been here before, in other words, in December 1973. As I walked, the road got steeper, and the centre of the city was falling away to my right. The houses were of moderate aspiration, all old but mostly in good repair. It seemed right, and I kept walking.

In 1973 I had hitch-hiked up to Launceston, across to the east coast, and down the east coast and back to Hobart. I had met the same people again and again, because I had stayed in youth hostels. We became friendly. When I got back to Hobart it was New Year's Eve, and some of us met up and had a great evening. Some of the people were staying at a shared house near the city, and I was invited to visit them the next day, New Year's Day.

This was the house my sub-conscious was trying to find. I felt that the house was on the left-hand side of the road, and not quite at the top of the hill. The house had been close to the footpath, but not right at the edge of the footpath as some of the houses were. There had been a front room with big windows. I kept walking. I thought I recognised it.

I walked a bit further to see whether another house might be more like it, but there was a Catholic school right at the top of the hill, so I walked back, and spent a while straight across the road, just looking again at this one house. I could picture the big front room,

32

the lounge room. On my travels I had been reading *The Electric Kool-Aid Acid Test*, a recent book by Tom Wolfe that recounted the psychedelic adventures of Ken Kesey and his followers, travelling across America in a colourfully painted school bus, trying to break through perceptions to see life anew with the help of LSD.

The people staying in the house were like that. Amid all the 'ordinary' adventures of travelling around and getting away from school, jobs, family, routines and predictable futures, there was a deeper, more uncharted venture going on in those days, and it was happening in this house. I had been in hospital for most of 1973 after a motor bike accident, and going to Tasmania was me back on two feet, walking and whole again. I had been on hold all year, and in danger for some of it, and now I was hungry for stepping outside the groove of normality. Tom Wolfe had fed the hunger.

I had kept a diary on my trip. I have never kept a diary generally; I don't know what I would say on a day-by-day basis. Hadn't James Joyce written a 600-page book based on a single 24-hour period of time – *Ulysses*? Doesn't that make the pitfalls of keeping a diary obvious? But I did keep a diary on my trip to Tasmania in December 1973. Further, I hadn't looked at it since. But before I went on this trip, I pulled the diary out and reread it, and then typed it up and read it again.

It made me feel things. What? Sorrow? Regret? Envy of who I was then? Gratitude for the richness of those experiences? Many things. I think that one thing was I was probably trying to emulate Tom Wolfe, as the immersed journalist. But I never tried to do anything with the diary after I came home. I simply put it away in my box of writings. Reading it again, I think there were moments that stirred me up too much at the time, and I didn't want to parade that diary in front of people – they might ask me questions that disturbed me.

And now, to bring out the diary at this point, after I have seen the house again, forty-six years later, I have reservations. However, I have seen the house, and it is still there, intact and one assumes it is leading another life, looking out over Hobart, and I am prepared to share that part of it – New Year's Day, 1974.

New Year's Day, 1974

I went back to where Donna and Olga are staying, in a scrappy-looking house that climbs up the side of a hill near the city. There were big hugs, smiles and questions all round. What have you been doing? (The funniest question; it was only last night when we were all together celebrating New Year's Eve!)

I turn around to look at this house, although it is a freak's house that we have all seen before, a potty conglomeration of miscellaneous paraphernalia; the grass is hidden in the kerosene heater, there are rugs strewn about, and the books on the shelves defy categorisation. One of the occupants is a psychiatric nurse, judging by some of the volumes. Another one paints, under inspiration, at undisclosed times, and the walls bear some of his work. It is beautiful, and sensitive, but avowedly schizophrenic. The floors and tiles are too homily strewn with candle-wax and used coffee cups.

The books are an assortment from William Blake to Dostoevsky, along with black magic and vegetarian recipes, and the *Women's Weekly*, of all things. There is a cheap record player, with Bessie Smith records, and Nina Simone, and J.J. Cale. Naturally.

Everyone is tired from last night, but talk ricochets sporadically about the room, about everything that has happened, at St Helens and since. Benjie is mentioned, and Magda, an Egyptian lady, and Tim, the Irishman, and Bill, who was succinctly known as 'the head'. Paul discloses that he thinks Benjie is psychopathic because when he talks, he can't get to the end of it without forgetting what he set out to say. I don't know what to make of this. What I remember is Paul saying, while we were at Bicheno, that in a sentence, Benjie remembers only the nouns, not the verbs, the relating words.

Paul claimed that he remembers the verbs in sentences, not the nouns. Psychopathy aside, this phenomenon made it hard for them to understand each other. Paul himself was hard to understand at times, but I didn't see this as being related to the expression of nouns and/or verbs. He had intense desires and an inability to keep them in perspective, or moderate them. He would start a sentence, then think twice about it and just leave it hanging, perhaps because it would have been embarrassing, or it was the wrong thing to say to certain people. Sometimes, he would finish the sentence and it *would* be the wrong thing.

Dear Paul. He and Olga were in the bedroom and I walked in. I think I was playing the role of circuit-breaker. Her face was in a pillow; he sat on the bed. In everything she did it was obvious she was fending him off, but he didn't or couldn't see it. And he asked me: "What do you think of our relationship?"

How I wished he had not asked me. I can never perform when I am put on stage like that. I never did my tap dance in the spotlight. I am sorry to say that I copped out. If my mind had unfrozen, I would have said what I should have: "I have seen you both before – how many times? Paul, you are too intense, and Olga can't handle that intensity. She is not even sure what she wants yet, so she keeps everyone on the surface of her life." But who knows if that would have been right either?

We all went out and said hello to the artist, Mike, who, however, was stoned and uncommunicative. I wonder how he will survive in Hobart, between the police and the small, country-town mentality?

Paul cross-examined him. He read his poetry (I avoided doing so). Paul addressed all of us: "Are all artists as strange as he is?" and then turned to Mike: "Are you lonely? Do you work?" and pointing at a line of poetry: "Why did you write this line?"

I remember that Paul had told us he got arrested last year and was fined $100 for sticking his thumb up at a policeman – insulting a police officer and resisting arrest.

Donna turns on Paul: "At St Helens, you tried to take over everything, like the Christmas food shopping, and the menu. You ordered people to get flour, and paprika. You even picked out the lettuce. You even told Olga we didn't need the loaf of bread she had picked out."

Paul walks out of the room. Olga is still standing there, and I know Paul wants Olga, but it is a stalemate at the moment. The artist has been forgotten. I think Paul has been remembering the verbs but not the nouns.

Donna is in need of a distraction, perhaps just to rescue Olga. Perhaps that has always been the point. So we go back to talking about hitch-hiking. Donna recounts some of the scenes she and Olga have played out on their pick-ups. They are instant theatre. Bored with repeating the same old life stories, they began to invent new characters for themselves. They became Emily and Jennifer from the USA, complete with accents: "Oh, yes, we lo-o-ve it here. We'll probably stay a-wh-i-le."

Or, once they were from Alice Springs: "Ain't she lovely, eh?"

They include a tell-tale slip of the tongue. It was not often detected: "Hey, Donna! Look at the view!" "Oh, Madonna, Madonna! The view! The view!"

But Paul is not to be distracted. He is instantly back trying to drag out the real history, from Donna this time: "How old were you when your mother died? Why did you hate your new mother?"

Me, I think Paul is digging in the wrong place. I think back to nights ago, when I thought he was hearing the words, but not their meaning. I say to him, "Sometimes, you just have to accept the view. The view! The view!"

Olga, ever impetuous, goes to the shop and brings back a crayfish. Of course, it is not enough for five of us, but we have the ingenuity of Paul on hand. We fiddled with soup, and potatoes, salad and omelettes at the stove. True to form I washed the dishes. Donna made the joke: "You look cute; you'd make the perfect husband. Tra-la-la!"

Later in the evening, summer time and all, we had the fire going, and we only talked sporadically. Leonard Cohen was on the record player: "Susan takes you down to her boat by the river.... and Jesus was a sailor." It is up to us to be faithfully impetuous.

There was no neat denouement to the evening. I had to drag myself away.

You can't talk about plane trips. You just get put in at one end and let out at the other. I came out at Sydney. When I arrived, it was so large that nothing else existed. Least of all were there any encounters between virtual strangers around an old crackling fireplace.

* * * * *

I had to show Lilian, of course. It took a while for her to respond.

"I could ask you the obvious question: Are you sure that was the house? Memory can be fickle."

"You could, but you're not going to...?"

"It doesn't matter. The street and the house obviously triggered something that's still there in you, after all this time."

"Yes. It's not as if I had the idea of looking for the house. I simply followed a sense of knowing."

Lilian said, "I think that, in a quilt there are many squares, and in some of those squares, things happen and then they unravel, and you have to gather the threads again to make new squares."

"I came away with a sense of loss from that day, or something unable to be fulfilled."

"Yes." She was quiet. "But a quilt is made up of many squares."

And that was it; that was our conversation.

Square 8

I rang Lilian. Yes, we had been communicating by phone while I was in Tasmania, and I had been sending her pieces to read. After dredging up the fragment about the house from my old diary, something else triggered.

"Do you remember me losing my glasses? And when I went back to the café the next day, the proprietor had them there waiting for me?"

Yes, she remembered.

"Well, I think he comes from my 1973 diary. I think he is a person who featured in that diary."

"That would be a strange thing. Why don't you write it down and explain it?"

"Yes, yes, of course. But I think it's him. It fits!"

"Okay."

* * * * *

The squares are beginning to overlap. That time when I was hitch-hiking, I got to St Helens on the east coast on Christmas Eve. I found the local youth hostel and checked in. There was a person who was the housekeeper of the hostel. He was tall and fair-haired, with glasses, not Australian, but an American Jew. A few Americans had started to turn up in Australia around this time. It was ten years after President John Fitzgerald Kennedy had been killed, and the United Sates was deeply involved in the Vietnam War. Some of their young didn't like the way their country was headed, and I didn't blame them. Australia's involvement in the Vietnam War had formally ended in January 1973. It was a good time to be in Australia if you were American.

Extract from diary, 24th to 26th December 1973

It was Christmas Eve, and we were all staying for Christmas now. Paul had taken over as kitchen master. He organised the collection of money for food, and we bought a big turkey and everything else Paul and others thought we needed. He said he would be in charge of the kitchen, but we must help him. We all agreed gladly.

Evenings were of talk-talk. When you put people together, they have opinions. They might even generate them spontaneously. And when you are on travels, there is always plenty to talk about – what you saw today, what happened on the road, what has happened between people, and what you think may be happening between people. "How do you say 'I like you' or 'I love you' when you only have one word?" I didn't know. I discovered a chess board and a willing companion, Olga. For our purposes, the question was not critical, but we talked anyway, while we were playing.

We laughed more than we concentrated on the chess pieces, but we managed to get through a game. From the kitchen I noticed Paul's eye on Olga. I had learned that Olga was a recent social work graduate. I was glad I didn't have to get involved in opinions about social work. I was starting to see myself as a radical outsider, and I thought it was best for that to be undisclosed. Yet, at another time during the day, I wrote: "Olga can be petulant and frivolous, but to use the corny expression, I think she has 'uneasy depths to her soul'".

Christmas Day. I went down to the bay in the morning and had a swim. Was that my first time for many months? Everything was quiet in this place. It felt like a sanctuary from Sydney, as if we were in a time before anyone had discovered it and wanted to make it modern. Tasmania seemed like a boy holding his breath while you walked past, and hoping you didn't see him.

Dinner was beautiful, a real banquet, with turkey, leg of lamb, potato salad, green salad, dumplings and cabbage, spiced rice, and cider. Paul was Czech. There was a group of ten of us, all sitting around on the floor, a joyful throng of personalities, no longer entirely strangers. Everything went so long that night, talk, laugh, sing, smile, hum – it rolled around the circle and round again and gathered us all up. We were people from all over the world, with accents, experiences, cultural niches, desires and curiosity, fresh from university, travels, jobs and family homes. Ranting, philosophising, sometimes laughing, sometimes too serious.

At the head of the table sat Benjie, the acknowledged father of the throng. He was the housekeeper here, an American Jew with an appropriate accent, who would need contemporary jargon in order to be described adequately. The extraordinary thing about him was the unanimous acceptance of his position at the head of the table, from all nations present, while around him whirled the vortex of opinions – David Hume and Jean-Paul Sartre, theories of truth and illusion – is it traditional, is it about complexity? Oh, the struggle of it!

Afterwards I wondered where all the words went. I imagined them still vibrating silently in the room, or up against the glass of the window peering out. It had been a very late night. In the trail of it, I remembered one phrase I heard: "the day's honesty".

I left in the morning before most people were up, and on the road I got a lift within ten minutes, all the way to Bicheno. I thought it was best that way, not to risk anything spoiling the day before and the night before, like awkward good-byes. But at Bicheno I was joined again by some of the crew from St Helens.

* * * * *

Benjie. It fitted. An American in St Helens, who had been here since the seventies, who had become part of the local community. Tall, glasses, the fair hair now grey, still sporting a beard, although now it was clipped close, but the pony tail told you there had been a free-flowing past. Presiding over his café the way he had presided

39

effortlessly over the table at the youth hostel on Christmas Day 1973. He had stayed.

What if I had known this when I was at the café? I could have asked him to confirm it. But it didn't happen that way, and it didn't have to. It fits, it makes sense. Now I remember that, the night I was at the motel without my glasses, I listened to music, and the album I listened to was an old one, from 1971, by David Crosby (one of many American musicians who sang against the dominant political forces of the day): "If I Could Only Remember My Name". It is an album that brings you back to earth, the gentle earth, away from the cruel affray, crowd politics and the posturing.

Square 9

I felt that I also had to come back to earth. Synchronicities are powerful, and remind us that energies resonate across time and space, and it behoves us to be aware and loving in our conduct. But spending your time looking for resonances in your experiences can be exhausting. Ironically, it defeats the purpose of living, which is always in the present tense. Accordingly, living is only ever about appreciating what is.

On my journey down the east coast, I made a point of stopping periodically, just to look at the view. I did not make a study of oceans and forests and bays, I simply stopped to look at them, and listen to the water and the breeze. I listened long enough to feel it flow through me, not expecting anything else. I jumped from rock to rock just to see what was there – plants that surprised me, the shapes and the colours of rocks, an abundance of flowers (remembering that it was spring and this is what happens in spring), and the soft lap of waves against the sand, all the way across the water from New Zealand.

I suppose we need knowledge in order to deepen our appreciation. Of course, I couldn't see New Zealand, but I knew that the closest shore to the east was the southern island of New Zealand.

And here we are back again, wading through our knowledge to find experience. But the waves go lap, lap, and spread on up the sand, again and again. And that is what is etched into the memory of the beach – lap, lap, lap. And it is beautiful.

I sit, and the sun comes and goes, flirting from behind the skirts of clouds, and it brings me to time, because this moment changes even as I sit. The present is slipping into the past. To enjoy the present is not to hold it still, it is to see that things are always changing. The wisdom that tells us to sit still ignores the fact that the present is changing. In this place, the person who sits still sometimes gets wet. Better to live in harmony, and seek the shelter of the car when it starts to rain.

Nevertheless, people make plans and suffer the consequences. It is good to stop the eternal rush, the endless quest for what ultimately does not matter. Sometimes it is better to miss a meal than to eat while you are running. Or stop running. We can underestimate how long it takes to stop. We think we can turn it off and on, at will, but a car remains hot after we have stopped the motor. If I put my hand on the bonnet, there is a lesson there. If I want to experiment, I can time how long it takes for the bonnet to cool, and then think about me, and how long I take to cool from various exertions, or from life quests for meaning.

I stopped at Coles Bay on the way down the coast, just to stop again and see what it was like there. I went into a café to get some food, and a young man with long hair was talking to the girl behind the counter in the café. He said he had spent the night before at the Friendly Beaches, and there was no one else there. It had been a lovely experience. She knew the place. I ate, and then walked around the headland. There was a beautiful view of the series of mountain peaks along the spine of the peninsula.

You can look at things and try not to think thoughts, but eventually your mind wants to get into the act. You think about whether you've seen something like this before, and where that was, and then you start comparing the two. If this doesn't work, and the place is natural scenery (that is, without buildings), you start thinking about being the person who is seeing it for the first time, whether that's an Aborigine, or a European explorer in a sailing ship three hundred years ago. And if you were the latter, you would be thinking about whether you'd seen something like this before, and where that was.

However, whichever role you take, your mind does come back to one thing: is it beautiful? And you begin to describe it, as if you were going to tell others what you had seen, and you had to try to get it right. And all the time you are doing this, the water is lapping among the rocks, the sand is even, the seaweed among the rocks is waving backwards and forwards, the sun and the clouds are still playing in the fields of the sky, and a tiny bird is darting backwards and forwards out over the water, and when you pay attention to it, you realise how fast it is flying.

There was a small island about five hundred metres off-shore, small enough not to attract any human construction. It was covered with stunted bushes, as befitting the storms and winds it was subject to. Perhaps it was a spot where fishers went to drop their lines successfully. I imagined that island, too – I would have a small bark hut and I would sleep on the island sometimes, paddling out there in my canoe, coming back with an armload of fish for my people, and grinning.

I imagine the artist at Salamanca markets reading my description, slowly. When I left Coles Bay I drove slowly, knowing what I was leaving behind.

Square 10

I sent my latest pieces to Lilian. I expected her to rake over them. Maybe there were bad stitches.

However, she thought I had probably summoned up a real connection from the past, and I was probably the only person on the 1973 trip who was keeping a diary, unless Benjie was. But who was Olga?

I answered, "A chess player, although not a serious one. Paul was the one who was more interested, and I don't know what happened there."

"And what about Donna?"

"You're teasing me. And there were other girls around anyway. It was a rich tapestry."

"Where did they all go?"

"There were two German girls. They probably went back to Germany. I think Paul was planning to head to Sydney for a while, to plan his move back down to Tasmania to build a cabin. Donna and Olga, I think they were headed for a Sydney beachside suburb, like Bondi."

"So you could have kept in touch."

"I was about to move in with a girl. She was upset enough that I had gone away without her."

"So why did you go away without her?"

"Because I had been cloistered for the best part of a year, in hospital, and I wanted to prove I could stand on my own two feet again – literally!"

Lilian listened. "But were you tempted while you were away?"

"I was delighted, more than once, but I had no wish to pursue those delights. There's a word, 'velleity'. You don't hear it often. It's an old word. It means merely wishing something, without any effort to bring it to realisation. The girls I met in Tasmania, they were velleities, delightful but not to be pursued. I already had a world at home."

Lilian let it go, and said, "What will you do next? You have nine squares. That's an odd number."

"Perhaps I'm finished. That would give me a three by three quilt."

"That would give you a nice little table decoration. I think you should try for more."

"I'm not trying for a fixed number of stories."

"Well, you shouldn't have chosen the quilt metaphor. There's an order about quilts. It should be a rectangle when you've finished."

"It's okay, I have other stories in mind."

"I'm counting," she said. "Bring me more." And she added, "The stories should balance each other in some way."

I thought the stories so far were in pairs, but that is as far as I had got. I wondered if Lilian was already planning how the stories would fit together.

It was another day of natural wonders. I went on a boat tour at Bruny Island. It wasn't a quiet little row boat or a putt-putt outboard. It wasn't a staid affair with a captain standing at the wheel chewing on a pipe. It was a blow-up boat with outboard motors that thrust you forwards at forty kilometres an hour. Although in local terms it was a very fine day, at forty kilometres an hour the wind was icy, and it took a week afterwards before the skin on my face had finished peeling off and renewing itself.

We had led up to the boarding of the boat in measured steps, all of which seemed nice and sensible. We started off in Hobart, checked names off a list and boarded a 24-seater bus. We drove south for about half an hour on a sunny morning. We drove through a town called Snug, which is ridiculous, and got to a place called Kettering, which is plausible. There we boarded a large ferry, I mean, the bus and a bunch of other vehicles got onto the ferry, and headed across the water.

Maybe it was a twenty-minute crossing. After we landed on the island, we drove to the north-east of the island, which took about an hour. We drove across a narrow isthmus between the north and south parts of the island; it was only about fifty metres wide. It's not every day you cross an isthmus. The bus stopped there, and you could walk up some steps to get to a lookout. I walked up the steps, about 120 of them. I won't say I was gasping for air, but I would be prepared to say my lungs were heaving. Which sounds worse?

It was after this that we boarded the boat, which took about twenty people, and we donned red rain-and-wind-proof ponchos, which also helped to keep out the cold. I sat with a lady from Hong Kong, 58 years old, married to a Hong Kong man for 30-odd years but travelling alone. She liked to talk and she had the capacity to enjoy things.

We travelled about 20 kilometres down the eastern side of the island, with New Zealand (not actually visible) on the left. The boat operators said it was a lovely day, calm and sunny, which meant that the swell was only about 1-2 metres. The boat skimmed right across it, occasionally smacking into the hollow of a swell and then flying upwards. But, all in all, it was remarkably stable and I didn't ever feel seasick. We were up in the prow of the boat, which moves up and down the most. The boat had a mixture of people – from various parts of Australia, and from China, Japan and India.

The island was all stone cliffs and forest. The rock was mostly dolerite, which is not quite like basalt or granite. It is grey-brown, and looks like it is stacked up in columns. Apparently it is very hard, close to the hardness of diamonds. That showed in some of the formations we saw, because there were columns that rose up out of the sea that looked like statues with faces. It was very beautiful. In one part of the shore there was sandstone, a much more familiar sight to me.

On the water line, there was a line of kelp all the way along, great armfuls of it washing about in the waves. This is harvested in Tasmania to make the seaweed solution you put on your garden to add minerals to it – the Seasol brand.

The forest above was quite thick in most parts, but in among the thickness of the trees were occasional white skeletons, much taller than the rest. These were the remnants of the bushfires of 7 February 1967, when bushfires swept across Tasmania in one day and destroyed about one-third of the entire island's forests, and 62 people were killed and 1,300 homes burnt down. (The bushfires that swept across Victoria in 2009 were also on 7 February, which I would call passingly strange.) It was quite spooky to see those white skeletons towering above all the new growth forest as silent reminders. Apparently it will be another eighty years or so before the new trees catch up to the height of the old bones.

We saw three caves on the water line, which go eighty metres or more inside the cliffs, and one cave that went under the water. How do we know? The waves rushed in and then blew out again in a plume of surf that went about five metres into the air. On a rough day, the plume goes many metres higher. It was a beautiful sight.

Our destination was to see a colony of seals on some rock islands about half a kilometre off-shore. They were there! We saw them! There were dozens of them, young bull seals lazing about on the rocks, enjoying the sun, preening themselves and swimming about. Mostly they were about two metres long. The mature ones can be four to five tonnes! We got very close, and watched them at play, and they swam about the boat.

45

On the way back, we saw many birds. One always hopes for whales, and we did not see any. But we saw a giant flock of shearwaters, which seem similar to seagulls, but black. They skimmed over the water, only about a metre above the surface. There were hundreds of them, some of them in a swarm sitting on the water, going up and down on the swell. But the most spectacular thing we saw was an albatross, sailing just above the water about fifty metres away. It was at least two metres wide, majestic.

We also saw a giant southern petrel, which apparently looked like diving straight down at the boat. I missed the magic moment and only saw a glimpse. The crew said they are a very aggressive bird, and they were obviously spooked for a moment. It can ram straight into other birds, and give them such a shock that they vomit up their food, which the petrel then eats. There are humans like that!

We got the bus back to the wharf, did the return trip on the ferry then drove up to Hobart again, getting back around 5 pm. That was an uncomplicated day, and a day of wonders. Sufficient is the day unto itself.

Square 11

I was thinking about my great great grandmother, Sarah Crosby, again. The place where I was staying in Hobart was just a few doors down from the church where Sarah and Edward got married in 1853. Although Edward was English, he and Sarah were married in a Roman Catholic church, the Church of St Joseph, which had been built in 1843. Somehow, Sarah's native religion held sway. I think that it must have meant more to Sarah than it meant to Edward.

One day I walked up to the church. The side door was open and I went in. It is a lovely stone church, a modest parish church, not a cathedral. Hobart's Roman Catholic Cathedral, St Mary's, was begun in the 1860s, and is a much grander affair. If the Church of St Joseph had more than a hundred people in it, it would be crowded.

Some of the embellishments in the church date from after Edward and Sarah got married, but essentially, the church is as it would have been then. If I try to imagine a traditional Irish church of Sarah's time, something that Sarah would have been familiar with, then I think she would have felt at home here. The pews, the vaulted windows (without the stained glass frescoes in 1853), the altar and the lectern, the dark of the roof timbers, she would have felt at home. The fact that the church had been designed by a convict and built mostly with convict labour may also have given her some wry satisfaction.

As I was standing there, an old gentleman came into the church. He put some brochures on the stand at the back of the church, either weekly news or an invitation to think about God in your life. I assumed he was the priest. I am sure he came in because he was wondering who I was, and what I was doing there. We spoke, and I told him the rather unusual reason for my presence here – the marriage of my great great grandparents.

He nodded. "That's a fine reason to come. They were difficult times. I hope that they found some joy in each other."

"I believe so," I said. "They moved to Sydney, and there were several children, including my great grandmother. So there is one small part of me that is Irish."

He smiled. "And there is one small part of you that is Catholic, that is, unless the Catholic faith carried on down your line."

"No, Father. My great grandmother married an Englishman, so that is the way things went. He was Church of England. But you may be pleased to hear that Sarah was buried as a Catholic, and I have visited her grave in Sydney. And Sarah Ann and Mary Susannah, two of her other daughters, are also buried as Catholics. Mary Susannah's husband was an Irish Catholic; Sarah Ann's husband was Scottish, but, like Sarah and Edward, they were married as Catholics."

"Ah well, I am sure that Sarah's faith was a comfort to her, and that of her daughters."

And with that, the priest thanked me for visiting, and I went on my way.

It was just a short walk that I was on now. I was on my way to visit the street where Edward and Sarah lived after their marriage.

It was only three blocks away. I wonder, on the day of their wedding, whether they walked that short walk from home to the church, dressed up for marriage and brimming with hope. No great carriage, no horses.

Watchorn Street is a short street, heading uphill from Liverpool Street to Bathurst Street. Would there be any sign of a humble abode from 1853? The Odeon Theatre is on the corner. I walked up the street, past a succession of commercial and industrial buildings, and a private car park, all depressingly modern and featureless. I got to Bathurst Street. Directly across the road there were two old buildings, with attractive stonework and chimneys, and a verandah with frills on the woodwork. At least, I thought, something is keeping watch over Watchorn Street from the significant days.

Sarah Ann and Mary Susannah, who were twins, were born in Hobart, in Watchorn Street. The other children were born elsewhere – Launceston, Adelaide, Sydney – and married outside of the Catholic Church.

This was as far as I could take this quest. I had been to the church where Edward and Sarah got married, I had been to the street where they lived, I had been to the Female Factory where Sarah had spent time as a convict, and I didn't know where Edward had spent his time as a convict. I had done my best to honour them, and I accept that all of the histories of our ancestors live underneath our skin. But there is likewise a need to live in the present.

I walked down the hill and towards the docks. The day was drawing to a close, and the light that washed across the streets now was a prelude to dusk. I came across a shop that hummed with life; it was a bar, although I am unsure about what words are used now. Once I might have called it a tavern, a place where beer is sold and drunk, but there is no accommodation. In the old days in England, it would have been called a beer house, which I like. The name of the place may have led me down that path too: the Dirty Penny.

It was all modern beers and close conversations. To drink here, one had to be able to distinguish between an ale, a lager, a pilsener, an IPA (Indian pale ale), a stout, a porter and a wheat beer. One had to know whether it was light, malty, sour, bitter, sweet or chocolatey. I doubted my capacity to detect the critical differences, but the ambience was cheerful.

All the men at the bar were bearded, with all manner of styles. There were full beards, neatly trimmed ones and exquisitely shaped ones. There was full black, wildly ginger and soberly brown, not to mention the multi-coloured samples. To someone who has worn a beard for most of his adult life but who is now clean-shaven, it was a little unsettling. Had there been some disjuncture in the great scheme of things, and we had been separated, and were now talking to each other across a gulf?

The man who served me was willing to help with the beer choices. He suggested that if I wasn't sure, a lager would be a good place to start. I could experiment with other types later. He told me his suggestion, which I readily accepted. It came with a good head of froth, and had colour that was jovial enough, not unnerving. I sat down to imbibe the atmosphere.

I wonder, how do young people live? Have they given up on the future and just spend their time cultivating a spirit of blithe enjoyment (namely, escapism)? Do they accept that the world is doomed, but think there is some secret key that will save us all (called technology)? Are they actually embarked on some venture that holds the key to our transformation out of doom?

I listened and watched. Of course, there is always the aspect of love and romance. In a world full of sorrow and foreboding, young people seek love, what the priest referred to as comfort. And then, being powerless about the bigger forces and where they are leading us collectively, there is some small joy. Could I see these dynamics at work here in the bar? Perhaps not, because people are good at presenting a façade; we need to. But I could sip and observe.

It was a Friday night, so many of the clientele had come from the office, with office trousers and shirts, and more ties than I expected to see, and the occasional suit coat. The ladies wore clothes that were mid-range smart, designed to show that you can present well, but not too showy. I think that Saturday night would be different. The talk gradually shifted from debriefs of office machinations to life outside of work. There was no frenzied drinking. I have to conclude that when you choose your drink consciously, you drink it more consciously, and certainly, some of the talk was about beer.

I allowed myself two beers, and the second was an ale. I refrained from ordering a stout, although my father would have done that from the start. The conversations continued. More people came, and some left. There were meetings. One of those was family, an older uncle meeting up with a nephew in his early twenties. Another was likely a business catch-up. There was a mixed group where there were no apparent tight connections to suggest couples. Conversation swam around the table, punctuated periodically with laughter.

The barman nodded to me as I left. I suppose I was seen as an old man in that context. I did not identify any incontrovertible evidence for any of my theories. This is the strange thing: there is such a schizophrenia about our lives. On one hand, it is apparent that we are doomed, with global resources running out and the climate warming dangerously. Everything our society does is overheated. On the other hand, most people live in comfort and they are nice to each other.

I also wonder about the differences between us and the generation in which Edward and Sarah lived. What happened to stop the harshness and heartlessness that characterised the transportation system? Are we different from the people of that time, and are we different permanently?

I had some dinner, fish and chips on a boat moored at the docks, and then walked along the docks in the evening. I found another bar, this time a light and airy place on one of the docks, with glass all around. It looked onto the water where boats were moored. There is something refreshing about the white hulls of boats bobbing in the dark blue of the water, all lit up at night time. I went in and ordered a drink, but not beer. I chose white wine, chardonnay. The bar tender, who had a neat, short-clipped black beard, was willing to talk about varieties and brands and regions.

A chalkboard sign at the entrance said this was a Jam Session. However, it was not like any jam session that I had been to. I was looking for some people on stage, and a gaggle of musicians on the verge, and maybe a chalkboard with names on it. What I found instead was a group of more than twenty people sitting in one big circle, all playing an instrument and singing in unison. There were very few people present who would classify as audience. The song they were singing was The Beatles' "Eight Days a Week".

I took my drink and sat near the back, seeking not to impinge on the circle. Most people had a guitar, but there were also ukuleles, mandolins, a bass guitar, a piano accordion and a piano. And most people had an iPad with the words of the songs on it. The age range was from fifties to seventies. Despite the Beatles' song, most of the songs they played were from the early sixties or earlier. I knew most of the songs; I even knew the words of most of them!

It was a quiet night for the bar tender. It was the songs that kept flowing. There were no individual performances, and no leader who stood out. One man announced the next song, but the lady on the piano was just as much in charge, and when a piano accordion plays, the piano accordion is always in charge. Everyone seemed to know what they were doing and were enjoying it.

I was sitting near a couple, and we talked quietly between songs. They looked like mature-age hippies, which is always lovely – these are usually the people who have sorted out how to make their way in life without giving in to a career in law or accountancy. They came from country Victoria, and they grew trees for farmers and ran workshops for farmers on how to grow trees. They had also been overseas, to Nigeria and East Timor doing the same thing, teaching farmers. The guy had a harmonica with him. He had seen the sign saying Jam Session and had come along thinking that he could join a band on-stage. But he played along to one song and he was good. They invited me to come along with them to a play the next night – their dose of culture in a different city – but I was leaving town the next morning.

Square 12

On another day I was at Ross. It is a small town with a long colonial history. Governor Lachlan Macquarie passed through the area in 1811 and named it after a place in Scotland. It soon became an important stopover on road journeys between Hobart and Launceston, and developed into a wool region. By the time of Federation in 1901, the town had four churches and a variety of other stone buildings that survive today, and a stone bridge that is still in use. The Ross Bridge was designed by the Colonial Architect John Lee Archer and built by convicts in 1836, led by two convicts who were stonemasons, James Colbeck and Daniel Herbert.

The bridge has intricate carvings on its three fine arches over the Macquarie River, which were executed by Daniel Herbert. The carvings highlight the incongruities of the convict era. Herbert was a convict, but for his entire time as a convict in Van Diemen's Land he worked at his profession, and the carvings on the Ross Bridge were above and beyond the call of duty. He had worked on many government buildings in Hobart, including one phase of the Cascades Female Factory built around 1830. He had also been a supervisor of other stonemasons, for which he received a small daily payment.

His crime in England had been highway robbery near Manchester, four counts. He had been sentenced to transportation for life. Yet his convict record was clean, and he was in constant demand as a stonemason. Well, not completely clean – he was reprimanded on a few occasions for drunkenness and absence from work. He was eventually given a free pardon, and actually lived out his life at Ross.

Herbert never offered any interpretation of the figures he carved on the bridge. One of them was supposed to be the Governor of Van Diemen's Land, George Arthur; another could have been the Danish explorer and enigma, Jorgen Jorgenson, and another two may be Herbert himself and his wife. Sometimes the carvings are described as caricatures, but the authorities never attempted to obliterate them. It was as if forms of uneasy peace were fashioned between the public façade of life in the colony and personal, human relationships.

I had lunch in the pub, which was one of the old buildings, and then walked up and down the main street. While I was walking, two separate groups of cars turned up in town. The first group were cars of different makes that were all from the 1940s to 1960s. These people conducted their recreation frugally, and ate lunch in the park out of Tupperware containers. The second group were of a younger age, and all drove souped-up Mini-Minors and Mini-Coopers. They all stopped in a line in the main street and went looking for a bakery.

I walked back down the main street and up a short hill to see one of the stone churches – it had a lovely spire – and realised there were things to be seen down the other side of the hill. A sign pointed to the remnants of the Ross Female Factory. It was a couple of minutes' walk. The Ross Female Factory held around 120 women at any one time, and operated between 1848 and 1854. Sarah was not one of them, I knew that, but I thought I would learn more about the circumstances of female convicts in this place.

There were three classes of convicts: the Crime Class, the Hiring Class and the women who were kept in Solitary Cells. The female factory was also a lying-in hospital for women giving birth, and a nursery for infants and children. A few male convicts stayed at the female factory as well; they did heavy work such as carrying water, chopping wood and looking after the livestock. That seems to parallel the organisation of the Cascades Female Factory.

One building remains on the site, the Assistant Superintendent's Quarters. The rest of the site is bare, but with some indication of where the crowd of buildings used to be, and there is a partially reconstructed wall around the boundary of the site, a memory of the imposing brick and stone wall that used to surround the female factory.

Most of the women were described by occupation as being servants of some kind, and their crime was usually only their first or second offence, which is to say, they were not professional criminals. Yet the free population generally had little sympathy for female convicts. They were regarded as being of poor character, and also of less value than their male counterparts. Many were regarded as prostitutes and as sexually immoral.

Mostly they were aged in their early to mid-twenties. While housed at the female factory, they were subject to a strict regime that consisted of work, discipline, punishment and religious instruction. The probation system sought to reform the women so that they would gradually be integrated into free society. Prisoners had the opportunity to attend evening school to learn reading, writing and prayers.

Around this time, solitary confinement was used as a form of punishment and discipline. A solitary confinement cell was a small room with no furniture except a pot for the toilet. The convict was kept in complete darkness and silence for twenty-three hours a day, and the food was bread and water only. They were let out for an hour to exercise, but still could not speak or communicate with other convicts. A convict might be kept this way for two or three days, but often much longer, perhaps twenty days. It was hoped by the authorities that this would be sufficient to reform the women. I remember that Tasmania is cold for much of the year as well.

In the records I have for Sarah, she had one stint on bread and water for three days, which I understand to mean she was also in solitary confinement.

I look at the signs for what they say about the treatment of mothers and children, given that Sarah had a child while at Cascades. If a female convict fell pregnant while they were in service, they were returned to the female factory to bear the child and receive further punishment for their 'crime'. The sign said the "conditions were grim and the mortality rate was alarming. Cascades Female Factory alone lost some 900 infants to assorted illnesses between 1829 and 1856".

Ross Female Factory was lucky in that the superintendent was a medical doctor who took some pride in having a healthy environment. Nevertheless, over the seven years it was open, 64 babies and children died, of illnesses such as influenza, cholera and pneumonia.

What I was really looking for was what happened to the children that lived, and the sign offered some indication. After a forced weaning period, mothers were incarcerated in the crime class ward for six months, and contact with their child was strictly controlled. Lenient supervisors would allow mothers to see their child more often. At the age of three, the children were removed to the Queen's Orphan Schools in Hobart.

There I have it – Sarah's child may have died as a baby, or she may have been sent to an Orphan School while Sarah was sent back to a Hiring Depot. For me to find the baby, I will need to find whatever records there are for the Orphan Schools. That is a job for later.

In all this, I cannot help but notice that the superintendent, Doctor Irvine, was not an intentionally unkind man. He was more lenient than many other people in authority, and he sought to create living conditions that were healthy for the women. It was the beliefs that drove the behaviour of people and the system; the belief, for example, that these women were somehow bad and they needed to be reformed, and the beliefs about how reform could best be effected. The belief that lack of prayer was the problem, the belief that it was the fault of women that they got pregnant, and the belief that this was because of women's fallen ways.

At long intervals during the period that the convict system prevailed, however, there was the occasional recognition that if a system was based on an appropriate foundation of belief, then it would, in fact 'work'. In the end, the convict system of punishment and reform did not 'work'. It did not reform people, and it did not impart to them a sense that justice had been served against them.

Sarah did establish a solid life as a free person with Edward. They moved to Sydney and their children were brought up there. But at her death, it seemed necessary for daughter Sarah Ann to fabricate the information for her death certificate. Accordingly, the entire period that Sarah lived in Tasmania (or Van Diemen's Land, as it had been known when she was there) was obliterated. For the purposes of the certificate, Edward became Irish, and Edward and Sarah were married in Ireland, and migrated straight to Victoria, then went on to New South Wales. It fell to the daughter to paper over the past to protect her mother.

Square 13

"My!" said Lilian. "You have been busy!"

"I have been bridging the past and the present," I replied.

"Are you angry about the past?" she asked. "Sarah had a tough life, at least in her young years, as you've described them. And you could blame the Church, the British Empire, prevailing religious beliefs, the culture of entitlement among the wealthy, and the demonising of poor people. There are plenty of targets."

"We were there then, and we are here now. It is good to be clear about the past, but it is not healthy to be impaled by it. I am grateful for people who maintained their core of identity, and who now and then let you know that they still knew who they were, and they were going to stand fast on that no matter what."

"For example?"

"Well, Daniel Herbert, the stonemason. He says, 'Yes, I will accept my imprisonment, and yes, I will use my skills, because there is some satisfaction in it as well as a legacy, but I will put my personal mark on it'. So he carves the faces on the bridge, lampooning public figures of the day."

"And Sarah. What of her?"

"It's on her gravestone. After her whole life, even after the erasing of the sorry facts of her convict past by her daughter, she has this to say: 'Native of Waterford, Ireland'. She keeps that as the core part of her identity, and even her daughter allows it to be writ proud on her gravestone."

"Yes, I see," said Lilian. "What will you do next?"

"I am not done with history. In any case, wherever you go in Tasmania, the history is evident. It is not like modern cities that feel obliged to destroy themselves every few years in order to stay 'modern' and to erase any reminders of what life used to be like. There can be no comparisons; you always have to believe that life is ever-modern and always excellent. But the past has scars, and it's healthy to be reminded of that, not to get too complacent. And the past also has its noble moments, in spite of, or because of, everything. Without a past, we are not human."

Lilian was listening. We were still communicating by phone, so I couldn't see her, but I felt that she looked down at this point, pondering. "Yes, I agree. Travel well," she said.

* * * * *

As well as Ross, I went to Richmond, another old town on the road between Hobart and Launceston. At Richmond there is another stone bridge, built by the same two convicts and convict labour. It was built in 1823, is of similar style to the one at Ross. It has four main arches and a smaller arch at each end. This bridge is still in use as well, and is very popular with tourists, even though it does not sport effigies on the arches.

I stopped at St Luke's Church of England, admiring its beautiful stonework (sandstone) and beautiful proportions. There was a plaque in the surrounding gardens to commemorate the visit of Prince Charles, the Prince of Wales, and Camilla, Duchess of Cornwall, in November 2012, and the tree they had planted, which is growing well. I noted that this church was designed by John Lee Archer, the same person who had designed the Ross Bridge.

Many of the buildings in the town are vintage stock, brick and stone and quaintness. People come here from Hobart for morning tea and mementoes. I had morning tea at the bakery, along with young and old, Japanese and Chinese tourists, and a gang of cyclists, not young, colourfully adorned, and wiry. I went into a nearby art gallery which also sold books about Tasmania. The shop was run by a cooperative of local artists and craftspeople. They were making things that were exquisite. Life bubbles up.

I walked the short walk from here to the vintage gaol. The prison sits intact after nearly 200 years. It started in 1825, and buildings and a yard were added over the next fifteen years. It housed the gaoler as well as male convicts, and female convicts were also held here. The gaol was used at one point to house the convicts working on the stone bridge, but Richmond became a police district with a local magistrate, so persons guilty of crimes in the colony were kept here, and punished here.

The facilities included a yard and a frame to which prisoners were tied and flogged. The gaol also included cells for solitary confinement. Here, you could go into a cell and close the door behind you. It was dark, completely dark, and in area, not much larger than a coffin. In another cell, there was a mannequin crumpled in the corner dressed in the female prison garb of the day. Near her was a night bucket for her toileting needs. The floor was the original rough-sawn floor boards. From these cells, you would have been able to hear the cries of the men being flogged in the nearby yard. It would have been hard to sink much lower than this.

A doctor was present for floggings. If the person passed out, or was losing too much blood, the doctor would step in and stop the flogging. A tally would be kept of how many lashes had been 'administered', and the flogging would continue the next week, or when the doctor deemed that the prisoner could handle the rest of his punishment. Blood and misery. Governor Arthur aimed to ensure that order was kept in the colony.

I walked into one of the buildings, where the convicts had slept, crowded and with little bedding or blankets. In one part of the floor, an exhibit had been set up. Glass replaced the flooring, and a metre below, in the dirt, there was an assortment of objects – shoes, items of clothing, dead cats and children's playthings. They were buried there by the prisoners as decoys for witches and evil spirits. The aim was to lure them into voids from which they could not escape, thus protecting the inhabitants from harm.

This was the world the convicts lived in, trapped and helpless everywhere they turned, and subject to the marauding of evil spirits. This gave a new twist to the effigies on the bridge at Ross. Perhaps in that instance the stonemasons took charge and harnessed powerful people to their cause, to expel evil spirits from the locality. It meant that Governor George Arthur, and Jorgen Jorgenson and the like, the powerful people, were harnessed to do the work of vanquishing evil. And perhaps Governor George Arthur did not feel so powerful as to interfere with the stonemason's work. Perhaps he also was a little wary of upsetting the spirits unseen.

I had been in another hotel in Hobart where the spirits dwelt. The hotel was called the Hope and Anchor; it was an old building and the bar was lined with dark wood panelling, and ships' gear was pinned up on the walls – ropes, anchors, winches, cleats and the like. I ordered a beer and sat on a stool, listened to the hum of voices and let my eyes get used to the dimness of my surrounds. Gradually, in the corner of the room, the face of a woman appeared, hair curled around her shoulders, and two large breasts, an eerie gold in colour. After a while it became clear that I was looking at a giant mermaid with a skimpy shroud about her shoulders, otherwise naked. I realised that this is what Hope must look like when you are a sailor at sea in the midst of a violent storm.

I call it 'faith in what we do not know'. Nowadays, with our faith in what we are pleased to call 'science', we comfort ourselves with the notion that we are merely a chance combination of atoms and molecules. This is another form of 'faith in what we do not know'.

After seeing the Richmond Gaol, I think back to Sarah. I wonder about her personal contest between toughness and terror and faith. The priest at the Church of St Joseph said he hoped that Sarah found some comfort in her faith. But faith can make you strong, and faith can make you weak. The giant mermaid could be an expression of helplessness, or it could be an expression of power. Which is it?

The clues come from unexpected quarters. When I look back through the photos I took at Cascades Female Factory, in several of the photos there is a shaft of light coming down. In one photo I took of a rusty steel bed, one of the sculptures strewn around the yards, a shaft of light is coming down onto the bed. I know this is a technological quirk of the camera, but when I saw it, it took my breath away, and I think it would be churlish to dismiss it as nothing, or mere atoms playing a game of chance. Sometimes there is no time, and no distance, between any of us.

I do not think of weakness when I think of Sarah. I think of her as Sarah, Native of Waterford, Ireland.

I sent the square to Lilian.

Square 14

"So, you are asking questions now?" said Lilian.

"And answering them," I replied, smiling.

"How are your stories going, as squares in a quilt?"

"I am not thinking about quilts at the moment. I am just making the squares."

"I am thinking about a quilt."

"You can do that."

"Can I?"

I realised what I had said. Maybe I didn't want Lilian to be planning a quilt out of my squares.

"Maybe. I don't know. Yet."

"Meaning you don't know yet, or maybe you will think about it?"

"We'll talk about it."

"Keep sending me the squares. Please. I love reading them. And I want to hear more about Tasmania."

"Okay."

I was happy to.

* * * * *

I thought about what Lilian had said. What did I think about Tasmania, this time? I remembered the piece from my old diary, that Tasmania "felt like a sanctuary from Sydney, as if we were in a time before anyone had discovered it and wanted to make it modern". Where had I felt like that? I went back to the diary. It said:

"I hitch-hiked across to the east coast. It is among the hills and very beautiful. It has been windy, so windy that once this morning while I was waiting by the roadside for a lift, and the grass was blown wild, it looked as if the entire hillside was moving like fluid. The country was green, and the road took the shape of the hills. In the dark gullies there were forests of ferns. I saw an eagle carrying off a large rat, and I saw a small dead wallaby on the side of the road. After five lifts I made it to St Helens."

This time, I rented a car in Launceston and started to follow the same route as I had over forty years ago, across to the east coast and then south. On paper, it looks as if you can get from Launceston to St Helens in less than three hours. In practice that is not so, because the road is steep, narrow and winding. You go up into the mountains and then down into a dale, then you go up into the mountains again and down to the coast to St Helens.

There are regular logging trucks, the really long, double-load kind (I don't know why they call them B-doubles), and on the winding roads you can't see far ahead, so you have to drive cautiously. At one point, a truck came around the bend towards me and there was no room for me to proceed – he was using up half of my side of the road, so I had to stop dead while he negotiated the bend. I suppose if you're a local you get used to it.

The weather was overcast, but it was not cold, and it did not rain at all while I was driving. I stopped at a lookout which was only built last year. It gave a view right over the valley and showed you how it was like a giant bowl, green and bountiful.

I stopped at a small town about 11:30 AM to have a break and some morning tea. It is a small town. The Church of England seems to be the main denomination here. The first shops I saw were opportunity shops selling second-hand clothes. This makes me think of poverty and unemployment, but then again, I have friends who buy most of their clothes at op shops. It is a sensible thing to do unless you are into fashion.

I saw a sign of the times: an unemployment service. Life these days is so....modern. As I was walking past it, three women came out, all thirty-something, all in makeup and all dressed in black. They were deciding which restaurant to go to for lunch. They all had the smell of power and confidence about them, which they had clearly learned to camouflage with gestures of compassion.

I went to a café for morning tea, and discovered I was to be a guinea pig for rhubarb scones. The lady had made them for the first time this morning. She wanted me to tell her what I thought afterwards. The scones were beautiful, and with rhubarb, perfectly fine. My mother would have been pleased with the scones.

On this journey I was travelling on the same path as in 1973, through St Helens and down the coast, and I remembered moments from that trip. I had stayed overnight at Bicheno, and then hit the road again the next morning to hitch-hike. I got a lift quite smartly, with a young couple in a panel van. Here is the story of what happened then.

An incident on the road (1973)

I hitch-hiked out the next morning. I got picked up by a young couple in a dark panel-van, Steve and Beckie. They were travelling round slowly. I had to sit in the back on the mattress because there was no room in the front, but this was fine. They were friendly and both happy to chat. Then Steve called out, "We're stopping here," and I didn't understand what for.

However, I crawled out, and the three of us were standing by the side of the road and Steve was pointing to a high-railed truck disappearing over the next hill. "Peas!" he said gleefully. And sure enough, by the side of the road there were clumps of fresh peas that

61

had fallen off the truck. "These are the best peas you'll ever taste!" he exclaimed.

We started tucking into them. They were so sweet! "There's a canning factory down the road," said Steve. "These peas have just been picked!"

I got to Coles Bay that day with ease. Later I travelled onto Swansea and stopped there for the night. I met up with a couple of familiars and several unknowns. We went to the pub and drank beers because it was someone's birthday, and they were German. Amid chit-chat, I learned that Paul, the Czech, wanted to build a log cabin for himself in Tasmania, near Burnie. I wished him well.

* * * * *

On this trip, I didn't stay overnight at Bicheno. I stopped for morning tea and moved on. Why? One reason: because I had been there before, and this time I wanted to see places I had not been to. Another reason: there was a raw moment then, in 1973, which I wanted to leave at rest – taking my shirt off in the sun, all my scars on show. I was freshly back in the world after hospital, functional but decorated with a patchwork of scars, and I was only just learning to live with it. I had let the world see it from the lookout, both arms raised in affirmation.

Bicheno (1973)

When I got to the youth hostel at Bicheno, Paul turned up with Ute and Matina, the German girls, and he cooked dinner for us – macaroni, which was, of course, excellent. I washed up, happy to be the humble servant. Afterwards we went for a walk down to the beach to see if we could see penguins, but I was confused in the dark, and distracted with my ankle; it was stiff and sore. We came back without having seen any penguins.

The next day I looked around, walking. It was so quiet around the town, there was just birdsong and cicadas. I walked down to the Gulley Boat Harbour, and up to the Whalers' Lookout, and to the Blowhole. I stood on the rocks at the lookout and took my shirt off in the sun – all my scars on show. The coastline looked like it belonged to *Lord of the Rings*, with hazy forests draping the hills, and ents and goblins still populating the hidden places. The seaweed likewise evoked *Lord of the Rings*, great forests of it writhing around the feet of boulders on the beach as the waves swirled it around.

Paul turned up with his camera and started shooting the foray, the armies of seaweed locked in battle. We strolled back to the hostel and at night we talked. The four of us slept another night there. But already it seems as if my time is coming to a close. Soon I will be back in Hobart and heading home.

* * * * *

This time, travel was quicker, because I wasn't hitch-hiking; I had my own car. It also meant I could stay longer in places. I don't think I saw much of Coles Bay on my previous trip. I was more concerned about not getting marooned on the side of the road at the end of the day. This time I stopped and walked around the shore.

Square 15

I had to choose whether to go to Port Arthur or not. I had visited there in 1973; I could argue that I had already been. However, I suspected that a lot would have changed – there is a more serious interest in history now – so I decided to go. In any case, I was interested in what I would remember.

As it turned out, I only remembered a few things. I think a lot more of the site has been restored and opened up since 1973. The whole visitor centre is new, that's for sure. I remembered the bay, and the settlement being in the valley around that bay. I remembered the façade of the main convict building, the penitentiary, and up on the right side of the valley I remembered the house that was built for government visitors, because it was just the walls, all stone, and no roof or floor, and I remembered that there were many rooms, and there was a fireplace in every room.

I remembered the shell of the impressive church, very square on the ground, and looking down onto the valley and straight across to the convicts' quarters. I learned this time, on the tour, that the minister was a hell-fire preacher who fulminated for two hours at a time, and of course, that was the convict's day off. The minister was also later deemed to be mad when he went back to England. But he certainly hated the Irish and Catholics in general.

I didn't remember anything about the gardens, and there was nothing about them in my diary. The gardens lead up to the church and they are wonderful, acres of them, with a formal pathway going up the hill through the middle of it all, with flowers and shrubs on either side. And of course, it is spring, so the colours are vivacious. The last time I came it had been the end of December, and there would not have been so many flowers.

The 1973 diary said this: "The buildings from the convict era are in a state of ruin. Some walls stand, but the bricks are crumbling, grass grows where the floor of the mess hall used to be, the church building has no roof. The signs say, again and again: 'Not much of this structure remains.'"

So, some things have changed. The church is still roofless, and there is only grass beneath your feet, but there are bells, and a story. The church used to have a set of eight bells, which weren't there in 1973. They had been given out to other locations in Tasmania, but in 1995 they were returned to the site and to the church. But the eighth bell (the smallest one) is missing. No one knows where it is.

I went on a guided tour, and the guide explained the buildings on the site, and how the place worked as a business, and the harshness and brutality of the regime. Port Arthur was established in 1830, at the time when it was being concluded that Macquarie Harbour on the west coast was not viable, because of the extreme weather there, and its isolation. The latter was closed down in 1833. Port Arthur was at first a timber-getting place. Then coal was discovered nearby, and the place spawned all kinds of industry, including ship-building.

The guide talked about Eagleneck Peninsula and the guard placed there to stop convicts escaping off the peninsula. The guard included a line of lights at night, with savage dogs placed at intervals. I had stopped earlier at the guards' hut on the peninsula, which is only a couple of hundred metres wide. The guards' hut is a long narrow building. The location doesn't look comfortable. I learned an odd fact. During the 19th century, a girl came to live there as a five-year-old, and she stayed and lived there her whole life, until her seventies, when she became too frail to live alone. Maybe her father had originally been an officer who was stationed there; I missed that piece of information. Transportation to the Australian colonies ceased in 1853, and the dog-line across the peninsula became irrelevant. Fancy living in a place like that all your life, and that's all you know! It is isolated, desolate, and with a dark history.

In 1973, I had my schoolboy learning about this place. I wrote: "I knew it had been a place of exile for the worst of convicts. It was a place of hardship, savageness and cruelty, in an environment that was harsh much of the year." And I commented: "I didn't feel any sense of relish in the portraits of wickedness of these early English convicts and their keepers. It was tiring, it tired me like a sense of foreboding, but I knew it was just the dark past, a potent mix of horror and shame and the other corrosive feelings created by those kinds of experiences."

When I came here before, I didn't have any knowledge of my family history, so I didn't know I had a convict ancestor. But I am fairly certain that Edward Lewis was never at Port Arthur. Or am I?

What I didn't know in 1973 was that across the bay from Port Arthur there is an island, called the Isle of the Dead because that's where the cemetery was, and to the south of it there is a promontory called Point Puer. The island is tiny, and there must be hundreds of people buried there. But Point Puer, for a few years, was a prison for boys.

Point Puer operated as a prison between 1834 and 1848. It was the first dedicated prison for boys in the British Empire. Puer means child in Latin. Although there was a spirit of reform in the establishment of this separate institution, nevertheless, it was known to be a harsh regime, and the guards would not have been of the compassionate kind.

This opened up a new question for me. Edward was still a child – he was fifteen when he arrived in Van Diemen's Land in 1845 – and I don't really have any information about how he spent his time as a convict. I knew he was in Hobart at the end of his sentence; that's all.

At Point Puer, the boys were taught trades if they showed aptitude. Edward did not practise a trade in his later life; he had

65

become a special constable after his sentence ended, and then a detective. Later he became a legal clerk. Although he had been a child pickpocket in London, the remarkable thing was that he had been taught to read and write. I think this happened at an orphanage in London where he lived for a time. My theory is that Edward was kept around in Hobart during his sentence and was used to carry out administrative chores, because he wouldn't have been a great deal of use as physical labour, and it was a bonus having someone around who could read and write.

But, it is a question now: Could Edward Lewis have been sent to Point Puer? Are there records? I will have to find out.

I went on a short cruise in the afternoon – a boat goes around the bay and out near the Isle of the Dead and Point Puer, and you get a good look back at the Port Arthur settlement. It is a huge place. It was closed down in the 1870s, but in later times it was used as accommodation for paupers and the insane, many of whom had been convicts.

Also, the Irish political rebel William Smith O'Brien was imprisoned here. He was an educated man and was fighting for independence for Ireland. He was tried for treason and could have been hung, but instead he was sent to Port Arthur. He was kept separate from the other convicts (he would have inflamed them!) and was treated well, like a gentleman in exile. He had his own house overlooking the valley, and his meals were cooked for him. Later, he went back to Ireland.

Later, I did homework on O'Brien. I wondered about the genteel treatment of him. It came down to two possible reasons. One reason was that he was descended from the eleventh century Ard Rí (High King of Ireland), Brian Boru. The other reason was that he was schooled at Harrow School and Trinity College, Cambridge. So, either he was treated well out of superstition – you don't mess with the descendant of a king, or camaraderie – you can't treat an ex-pupil of a Public School badly.

There was another piece of interest in the 1973 diary. After my solitary tour of Port Arthur, I had met up with some of the people I had met at the youth hostels.

Reflections on Port Arthur (1973)

Strangely, I didn't meet up with anyone I knew until after I had completed my sombre tour of the convict site. It was after I got to the youth hostel that I met up with Paul and Ute and Matina ("the German girls") and some others I knew less well. We went down to the pub to eat and have a drink. In a group full of foreigners, I enjoyed a frank discussion of our convict past – what it looks like when you come from a country where this had never been a systematised method for dealing with people who were poor and whose crimes were mostly of a trivial nature, or related to food. Their reactions were disturbing to me. I had to contemplate the possibility that people not from a British background might see 'us' as more barbaric, historically, than their people were.

We were all a bit careful not to be too loud about these views. They knew they were in a foreign country, and I knew I was an outsider. We didn't attract any attention until a young Australian guy came over with his drink. I recognised him. He was a tourist guide from the convict site. He introduced himself as John. I wondered what his stance would be, yet he seemed happy to join us.

We needn't have worried. When Paul, who had no difficulty being outspoken, made a critical remark about the barbarity of Australia's past, John laughed loudly and said, "Working here, I've had plenty of time to think about all this. But remember, it's only ever a few people who are running the show. Most of the convicts were just focused on staying alive and getting out one day. They were at the end of the earth, and probably with no way back."

These were humbling thoughts, considering the nicely crumbling buildings and the lush green grass of the convict barracks site, as soft as an English spring. I was just sitting with my drink, thinking about this. I was glad when Ute and Matina suggested we go to a local dance. It was a proper dance, a dress-up show in the local hall, a Tasmanian up-country frolic billed as an Evening Spectacular.

Port Arthur has left us with a lot to think about.

Square 16

I wondered what Lilian would have to say about my square on Port Arthur.

She rang me. "No, it wasn't enjoyable stuff," she confessed.

"It wasn't meant to be. I can't reduce the Port Arthur experience to some fun bit of the distant past."

"I know."

"When I was at the Richmond Gaol," I said, "a family was looking around at the same time, and the mother was pointing out the cat-o-nine-tails whip to her five-year-old daughter. It was as if it were a quaint toy. She even remarked how this one didn't have the barbs on the ends of the thongs. I found that conversation chilling."

Lilian sighed, but she said, "It's still hard to know what to say to children. We don't want to hide the past or forget it, and we don't want to horrify our children, but what do you say to a five-year-old in a place like that?"

"We're no longer like that?" I suggested.

She laughed. "Or, 'It's complicated.'"

"In the leaflet for Richmond Gaol, it tells us about Solomon Bleay, who was transported for life in 1836 for making counterfeit coins. He became the colony's hangman and he executed over 150 people in his lifetime."

"Some people think we should still be doing that."

"But," I offered, "as John the tour guide said in 1973, it's only ever a few people who are making the decisions. Most people just want to stay alive and get out one day."

"We are a democracy," Lilian observed.

"It's complicated," I laughed.

* * * * *

I want a square for the larrikins I met in 1973. When life is hard, and the rewards seem to be distributed unevenly, some people seem to survive by extracting what fun they can out of the situations that life presents. In Australia, writers like Henry Lawson, 'Banjo' Paterson and C.J. Dennis depicted the larrikin as authentically Australian, characterised by non-conformism, irreverence and impudence.

I was hitch-hiking, and one is subject to the vagaries of traffic. Anyone might come along. It could be larrikins. I encountered a group of sheep shearers who had just finished a season in Tasmania.

Hitch-hiking in Tasmania (1973)

Monday 17 December. I picked up my first ride walking out of Hobart, on my way to the National Park, although I had to walk the last five miles. One of my lifts drove me on a detour up to a hilltop to see the view. The valley was full of hop plants on trellises.

Walking along the road, I had to take care because logging trucks were thundering down the road with load after load of logs, in a desperate effort to get as much timber out as they could. Soon, the original Lake Pedder would be submerged to become a much larger body of water created by three new dams that had been built in 1972. There had been protests from 'greenies', but the dams had not been stopped. [Current note: This was two years before Bob Brown rafted down the Franklin River and the Green movement started in earnest.]

Tuesday 18 December. I walked down to Russell Falls, despite my foot and leg being sore. I am still recovering. Waterfalls are necessary as sanctuary from the city, and we all need sanctuary sometimes. I got a ride in a Mercedes Benz strewn with Eskies, movie cameras, a stretcher, and suitcases. The man was on holidays, dressed in a sports shirt and slacks.

My most memorable ride was with some sheep shearers coming back from a season in a Tasmanian shearing shed. They were very drunk, and we weaved our way along the road, managing to miss fence posts and veer around rubbery bends. We got to New Norfolk, where they had to stop and have some more drinks. After spending most of this year in hospital after a motor bike accident, I could see the irony of my being a passenger in a car that was trying to get itself smashed up.

I waited for another lift, but when the shearers came out I was still there, so they picked me up again. We weaved along the road once more, to Tunbridge, they with a few bottles for sustenance, and managing to miss more cars and posts. I was sweating slightly and counting the milestones.

The shearers had a few more beers at Tunbridge, and then they suggested I go in another car. He was another one of their crew. He had his own car, a Mini-Minor, despite the fact that he was only fifteen and he didn't have the licence to go with it. I thought I was better off with him; he wasn't drunk. He got me to drive through the towns, because of the police, but he took over once we were out of town. I managed the clutch and accelerator pedals – I was still cautious with my recovering leg – but I said he had to drive because my foot couldn't take it for long.

The boy said he owned thirteen motor bikes and two cars. He'd just bought this one. He actually drove well, and he didn't play chicken with the posts on the side of the road. We got to Launceston, and I got off. They were on their way to get the ferry over to the mainland so they could drive back to Adelaide.

I found that Launceston was a town full of churches – white stone, sandstone and old brick, and bells. I walked down the track to Cataract Gorge, and then into a park with peacocks.

* * * * *

Are there still larrikins in Tasmania today? I think the nearest I came was at the lake with the shanty town of shacks. I am referring to the jovial sort of larrikin who is irreverent and cavalier, not the other type of larrikin who also turns up in Australian literature, who is rowdy and ill-mannered, who gets around in gangs and who may insult people, beat them up and steal from them.

I think the shack owners saw themselves as rebels who wanted to get away, and who wanted to create their own place 'in nature' that they had control over. In a patchwork quilt, they would own their own square, although it might not be quite square. It would be rough, idiosyncratic and comfortable. It might be themed on the colour pale blue, or on old fishing tackle. It didn't have to make sense, it just had to be distinctive, and owned.

And the larrikins would be prepared to defend their little bit of paradise, the cheerful anarchy of it. They are good at tolerating each other's foibles. They like it rough and they have no time for prettiness. They would rather be chuffing about in a boat than tending a garden. They don't seem to mind all the dead trees sticking out of the water.

They are suspicious of outsiders, but they look for tell-tale signs that you might be acceptable, and tell-tale signs that you aren't, and if the latter occurs, the atmosphere gets perceptibly chillier. It wouldn't come to blows or thuggery, but you would know it was time to leave sooner rather than later.

On the west coast, I came across the other sort of larrikin. The difference was belligerence. It was a bush premises for people who liked to ride around the beach-front bush on dune buggies. The clue about their attitude was in a roughly painted sign on a large sheet of steel, hand brushed in black and red. It said the country was for 'MULTI-USE', and this word was written in all caps and in red. What it meant was, they could ride everywhere in their dune buggies and do donuts in any patch of grass they came across. They could set traps and take all the crabs or anything else they chose. Of course, you were free to do that too, although one suspects that you weren't, not anywhere in their vicinity, anyway.

Yes, there are still larrikins. I think Henry Lawson and Banjo Paterson and C.J. Dennis would have been able to relate to the sheep shearers. The shack owners would have been a bit too modern for them, but understandable. And the dune buggy marauders, likewise a bit too modern but sadly, also understandable.

Square 17

I was still keen to find what traces I could of Edward Lewis and Sarah Crosby, or Edward and Sarah Lewis, as they became. After the birth of the twins in Hobart they had a son, called Edmond in the birth register but called Edward Lloyd Lewis in all the records after that, the same name as his father (the father Edward assumed the middle name 'Lloyd' after his convict years, taken from his own father). After a couple of years in Hobart, Edward, Sarah and the children moved to Launceston. This was in the mid-1850s. In Launceston, my great grandmother was born – Ellen Elizabeth Lewis, on 24th October 1857.

The problem with the birth register for Launceston is that all the babies only have 'Launceston' for their address. It was Sarah who registered the birth, and the register shows the 'x' mark that people who can't write put instead of their signature. But how could I find where they lived? Currently, Launceston's population is over 60,000. It is a big town.

The solution was simply to walk around, and look at old houses and buildings, and to take in the town (it was declared a town in 1852, and a city in 1888). The first white people in the area were George Bass and Matthew Flinders, who were sailing around the coast of Van Diemen's Land in 1797 to try to prove that it was an island, separate from the mainland. They took shelter at the mouth of the Tamar River during a storm, and sailed up the river as far as the current site of Launceston. A settlement was established at the mouth of the river in 1804.

The Launceston area quickly became a grazing area for cattle and sheep, and a port for goods being exported to Australia and England. By 1827, the town's population was 2,000, and hotels, churches and government buildings were being built, and the town kept growing. When Ellen Lewis was born in Launceston in 1857, the town's population was heading towards 10,000. I accepted that I wasn't going to find the family's particular house.

Moving to Launceston may have been Edward and Sarah's way of distancing themselves from their convict pasts. It must also have been known to them that in the late 1840s, the Reverend John West, a Congregationalist Minister from Launceston, had founded the Anti-Transportation League, and written a charter to abolish the shipping of convicts from England to Australia.

Reverend West played a major part in the movement to end transportation, widening the base of the movement to all Australian colonies in the early 1850s. He toured and lectured for the cause and spoke at conferences, arguing that transportation was morally wrong. By the time Edward and Sarah arrived in Launceston, West had moved on to Sydney to become the editor of the *Sydney Morning Herald*, but his movement had gained huge momentum.

In fact, the last convict ship to be sent from England was the *St Vincent*, Sarah's ship, on another trip in 1853. How my family history would have been different if Sarah's boat had not come to Hobart Town in 1850 and she had not met Edward!

My tenuous hold on a connection with Edward and Sarah and their four children in Launceston comes down to visits to places that would have been there in the late 1850s. I stayed next to the Cornwall Hotel, which was first established on the site in 1824 and which was Launceston's leading hotel for many years. It was the venue for the meeting where the Anti-Transportation League was established, and it was where the first meetings of the Municipal Council were held in 1853. The publican, John Pascoe Fawkner, was also one of the founders of the Melbourne colony in 1835, along with John Batman.

Did Edward drink there? I can only say this: that after Edward and his family left Van Diemen's Land, he became a detective in Sydney, and in that role he would go to local hotels to 'keep his ear to the ground'.

I went to Cataract Gorge, which has always been a place of recreation, right from Launceston's early colonial days. Did Edward and Sarah take their young family there? The earliest recorded visit to the Gorge was by the settler William Collins in 1804. About his visit he wrote: "Upon approaching the entrance I observed a large fall of water over rocks, nearly a quarter of a mile up a straight gully between perpendicular rocks about 150 feet high. The beauty of the scene is probably not surpassed in the world". I picture Edward and Sarah with their children playing here, enjoying the beauty of the place, both free citizens now.

In the 1890s, a turbine-driven power station was constructed further up the river, and Launceston was the first city south of the Equator to be lit by electricity generated by water power, from December 1895.

I also went to the Royal Oak Hotel, which was built around 1850 and is still in business. I discovered that the name Royal Oak comes from a story about King Charles II back in the 1600s. During his years as a fugitive from Oliver Cromwell, the king once hid in an oak tree at the house of a loyal subject. The tree began to be referred to as the Royal Oak, not as a symbol of defeat, but instead, one of defiance and loyalty to the kingdom.

I went to the Royal Oak for a drink, and for dinner, and to listen to a singer. I was keeping my ear to the ground for new music, and it was a good night.

Apart from this, I walked in the City Park, among trees that go back to the 1820s. The park was an early thought in the minds of the settlers, with land set aside for a botanical garden in the 1820s. Accordingly, some of the trees in the park are well over 200 years old, which tends to put your own life into appropriate context. I think that the light plays more extravagantly with old trees. It could be a trick, but I don't think so.

Edward and Sarah did not have the opportunity to enjoy the glasshouse. It dates from 1932; but they would have loved it, and the children would have been enchanted. Even more so, the children would have been enchanted by the macaque monkeys, a gift from Ikeda City in Japan in modern times. That's the nature of looking at the ancestors – they are so far, but then they are right at your shoulder, close. Something strange happened in Launceston, because one minute, Edward was a labourer (as evidenced by the entry for baby Ellen in the birth register), and suddenly he is a detective in Sydney, and the family has moved.

The flowers in the glasshouse look even more beautiful. Moments in time. And walking near the macaque enclosure I see the wisteria vine in full bloom, and read that it dates from 1837. If Edward and Sarah strolled here one day with the new baby Ellen, it must have seemed like a miracle, like being thrown up on a beach when you thought you were going to drown at sea.

Square 18

"The larrikins are a backdrop," said Lilian. "It's a question of whether they are there all the time, or whether time changes and they disappear."

"Henry Lawson would have asked that question. He had his affections," I said.

"Well, I'm not going to tell you it's a better world," she replied. "It's shinier, and there's more concrete and glass."

"Is it technique that creates gardens, or love?"

"I'm voting for love."

"I'm voting for time. Technique can't invent a 200-year-old tree."

"Do you expect to get any clearer about Edward and Sarah?" Lilian asked me, attentively.

"I do," I replied, "Little by little, or in strides."

"What does a stride look like, or is that unfair?"

"Sometimes, I think that Sarah was not so alone. For example, I had another look at her and Edward's entry in the marriage register. One of the witnesses to the marriage was Mary Tyrrell, and I looked her up in the database of the Female Convicts Research Centre. Edward and Sarah got married in March 1853, and Mary had been transported only six months earlier. She was Irish, from County Clare. But she was 56, and this was her first offence – stealing a sheep. She was a widow.

"It was the norm of the police and legal worlds of the day to consider people like Mary Tyrrell to be 'of the criminal class', but when a 56 year-old widow with no previous convictions comes before the court for stealing a sheep, something in the scheme of things is broken, or ripped out of shape.

"Sarah must have met her at Cascades Female Factory. I put these pieces together, and I think Sarah found some comfort with the older lady. She could have been like a mother to her. And there is Mary at Sarah's wedding at the Church of St Joseph, being a witness to the marriage. Mary herself got married the following year, to a man by the name of George Carrington. There was benefit in a woman getting married, because that effectively ended their servitude as a convict. One hopes that Mary got lucky, and found a nice man.

"So, yes, this was a great stride in my perception of Sarah's life. She may have been cut off from her homeland, and destined to spend the rest of her life far from Ireland, but connections turned up. Yes, I always expect to get clearer about Edward and Sarah."

"How is your trip going? How's Tasmania?"

"Well, I know that Edward and Sarah left around 1858, probably to go directly to Sydney, so I am thinking about whether they were drawn to Sydney or pushed out of Tasmania."

Lilian said, "Most convicts left Tasmania. They tried to leave their convict past behind, didn't they?"

"Yes, that seems to have been so, and I have concluded that from Edward and Sarah. But I also think Edward was pursuing opportunity."

"What's next? In Tasmania today, I mean."

"I know what you mean, and I have been to places that I loved, but I am still beguiled by the past. We come from it and I feel the need to understand it. And there's actually another branch of the family."

"There is?"

"My mother, who was an Archer, always said, 'There were Archers who went to Tasmania, you know.'"

"That sounds conspiratorial."

"Yes, it sounded a bit like a secret. But I don't think she knew anything more than that. I also think that the way she said it mimicked how it had been said to her as a child."

"Well, what do you know?"

"Mum thought they had a title, barons or lords or some such."

"And have you found them? And do they have titles?"

"Yes, I have found them, and no, they do not have titles, but yes, it is a good question."

"Is this shaping up to be a square in your patchwork quilt?"

"It feels as if it should be a square. It has a place, and it is quite a story."

"I look forward to it," ended Lilian.

* * * * *

My mother always said there were Archers who went to Tasmania, and they were important people, lords or earls or something. It was said with a mixture of envy and disdain, that my mother had clearly imbibed from the person who had conveyed the story to her when she was a child. I was never interested in the story until I started doing family history, rather late in life. Even then, the story was too far back for me to consider. It took me four or five years of research before I was far enough back into the past to try making any connections.

The Archers of Tasmania were not hard to find. An historian (Neil Chick) has written two large books about all the Archers who have come to Tasmania. They were certainly a family of renown, and the family remains so today, and two of the properties they have owned are on the National Heritage register – Woolmers and Brickendon. And I am connected. My mother was right about that.

You could say that the story starts with William Archer (1754-1833), a miller by trade, in the English county of Hertfordshire. He was a successful businessman, a man with an entrepreneurial mind, who had five sons who lived to adulthood. He had travelled extensively looking for ways to expand his business, sourcing the best grains and equipment for milling flour. However, for all of the sons to have a future, they were going to have to spread their wings. Joseph and Edward journeyed to America, and Daniel travelled to India. In 1811, Thomas was sent to New South Wales, with a letter of introduction to the Governor of the colony. John Archer, the fifth son, stayed home.

Thomas was not long in New South Wales, for in 1813 he obtained a government position in Van Diemen's Land, and in 1817, Governor Macquarie granted him 800 acres of land on the banks of the Macquarie River near Launceston. Later, Thomas was joined by his brothers Joseph, William and Edward, and the father, William, also migrated to the colony. Between them, they acquired and farmed tens of thousands of acres of farm land. Thomas farmed Woolmers, and William farmed Brickendon.

Meanwhile, William the miller's brother John Archer remained at home in Hertfordshire. John's son, also called John, married Susannah Paternoster, and they had a son, Edward (among other children), who married Mary Clifton, all in the close confines of Harpenden, Hertfordshire, and they had a son called William Archer (born 1813). (The name 'Paternoster' turns up later.) This William, my mother's direct ancestor, is a significant person, because he is the one who pioneered the presence of the Archers in New South Wales, although his migration was involuntary.

This William Archer was charged in Middlesex Quarter Sessions in 1837 with stealing 28 pairs of 'high shoes' and the basket, or handcart, they came in. I believe it was in the vicinity of the White Horse Inn, which still stands today on the outskirts of Harpenden. And I think 'high shoes' are good-quality shoes made out of goat leather, made, not by a common cobbler, but by a cordwainer. And as it happened, William Archer had a cousin who was a cordwainer. William would have known the shoes would be desirable items, although tragically easy to trace.

Accordingly, my William Archer was sentenced to be transported to the colony of New South Wales for seven years. He was shipped out on the *Lady Palmyra* in 1838, and served his time on a farm in the Hunter Valley north of Sydney. It seems that he inherited some of the entrepreneurial spirit of the Archer family. He married a Scottish lass, Ellen Welch, and became a farmer in the Hunter Valley. However, after a few years of this he decided to do the thing that many ex-convicts dreamed of doing: packing up and going 'home', to show everyone you had made something of yourself.

At this point, it is necessary to know another of my mother's stories, namely: "There are no convicts in our family (meaning the Archers). We all came out here as free settlers." She said it word for word, with even the same intonation every time, from when I was a young lad to when I was in my sixties and she was in later life. I would never have contested her about this matter, and I never did.

When I was doing my family history research, I made contacts with people who turned up in other family trees, people in Australia and England who had been doing their own investigations, and it was said to me on numerous occasions: "You know, William Archer was a convict. He was sent out to the colonies to fend for himself." This was said mainly by people (in the great family web) who had never left England, and I received it with a wry smile. But they had the essential truth of it. William Archer (my one, the one who was born in 1813 in Harpenden) had been transported for the crime of theft of goods from the person.

So, the Archers (my side of the family, not the Tasmanian Archers) have given me a good laugh. William Archer (convict) packed in his farm and packed up his family and went back to England in the late 1860s. He bought a farm in Kent and farmed an orchard. Kent is very nice, but why not Hertfordshire? I have a theory. When it came to it, he realised that you can never justify yourself to the relatives. They have already dismissed you; they have cast you off as a rascal, or something worse. There is no redemption in the old world.

William has arrived back in England with money, but my theory is that the relations wouldn't buy his story. So he makes alternative plans, and he has his own redemption, and it is based on the kind of good, solid work that his relatives and ancestors would actually understand. But they will never acknowledge him, and this is why he is on the other side of the river, the River Thames.

Hertfordshire is to the north of London, Kent is on the south side. He buys land in Kent and establishes himself, one more time. Then, how does the story go? He realises, after a few more years, that there is nothing in this. No one cares. He might as well make his name in the new colony, and so he emigrates again, this time voluntarily.

The voyage 'home' had good omens. Firstly, it was a new ship; it was her maiden voyage – the St Osyth. It was a joint steam-and-sail boat that was envied for its speed; it managed the voyage from England to Australia in forty-one days, arriving in Sydney close to Christmas Day. The other good omen was the presence of twenty or so acolytes of Sister Mary McKillop, who only in recent years has been accorded the status of Saint in the Roman Catholic Church. She had been on a recruiting expedition in the British Isles to find passionate young ladies who cared for the welfare and education of children in the colonies. She had been successful.

When William stepped ashore in Australia again, he was a free settler. The past had been erased. When Ellen, his wife, stepped ashore, she signified the event by changing her name to Hellen, and was ever-after known as such. The name Helen has then been carried on through the generations.

William had a mission too. It was not farming. That was the mission of the other branch of the family, the lords and ladies of Van Diemen's Land. No, his mission was to be a publican, to have his own hotel. Perhaps it was because his father had at some point been a brewer (true), or perhaps it was simply because he had spent a goodly amount of his time at the White Horse Inn in his youth. Perhaps he would have liked to have been part of that establishment.

William had not been ignorant of the other branch of the family. He heard about things that happened, things that turned up in the news. While he had been in Kent, he had heard about the visit of Queen Victoria's son, Prince Alfred, to the Australian colonies. It was an eventful six months. (How the Royal family must love air travel! It means the trips are shorter.) For one thing, Prince Alfred had been shot while in Sydney, by an Irishman who wanted independence for Ireland. The Prince recovered from the bullet wound to the stomach. The Irishman was arrested, tried and found guilty, and although Alfred pleaded for clemency for his assailant, the man was promptly hung. British justice was efficient in the colonies, and it was recognised that the sons of Royals could be a bit soft.

Prince Alfred also visited Tasmania, and once there, it was necessary that he should acknowledge the accession to establishment status of the Archer family. He had dinner at Woolmers. But while at dinner, he mischievously determined to carve his initials into the edge of the dinner table, which was a formidable, ornate thing (for this locale, anyway) that could seat twenty people. Not to mention that the table was adorned with the Archer dinnerware which was decorated with the newly devised Archer crest. The crest depicted the forearm and paw of a bear (for strength), with the paw thrusting aloft and shaped as a hand grasping an arrow (for the Archers).

There must have been moments of discomfort among the party about the Prince's vandalism – such a conflict of expectations and clash of mores, but Alfred declared his crime delightedly, and it was greeted with gracious (obsequious) colonial humour. If you go on a tour of the house today (which I did), you can still see it.

I think William Archer (mine, the convict) knew all this. In 1890, when he opened his new hotel in Harris Street, Ultimo, it was called the Duke of Edinburgh Hotel – Prince Alfred's title. Moreover, he had something in the hotel that celebrated the White Horse Inn. Was it a statue, was it a painting? I don't know. Research is not a done thing, a *fait accompli*. But if my mother was sure of anything, she was sure about this: there was a white horse associated with the hotel. So, there he was, William, doffing his hat to Royalty through the name of his hotel, and at the same time, giving a salute to the hotel where he had made mischief as a young man back in Hertfordshire. It was a high sign to the Archers of Tasmania, even if they never noticed.

There was another nod in the establishment of the Duke of Edinburgh Hotel, to William's grandmother, Susannah Paternoster. This end of Harris Street was just being developed at the time, and the little street behind the hotel was named Paternoster Row, and that was where the family lived.

Square 19

"So, to be clear," said Lilian, "the Archers of Tasmania did not hold titles such as lord; their beginnings were as businessmen, as millers of flour, but your branch of the family saw them as being a lordly kind of people?"

"I think all of the truth was contained in the way my mother said these things," I replied. "I even suspect there was an element of not taking yourself too seriously, but also, the spinning of a good yarn."

"Almost like a larrikin?" Lilian grinned.

"Yes, that helps," I replied, smiling. "And the Archers at Woolmers devised for themselves their own crest. This was obviously intended to suggest that the Archers were now in the class of lords or earls, or barons, as my mother sometimes said it."

"And you've never found the white horse, whatever it may have been?"

"The quest is never over," I said.

"Did you see the Woolmers estate?"

"Yes! The tour guide there told us about Queen Victoria's son carving his initials into the dinner table. That's when I put the story together with the story of William Archer coming back to Australia and building the hotel that he called the Duke of Edinburgh. I think you can't underestimate the power of human motivation – my William wanted to show himself up to the Tasmanian branch of the family. Maybe that urge went back two generations, to when John Archer was left back in Hertfordshire while all of his brothers were experiencing grand success in Van Diemen's Land."

"Yes, yes, it makes sense."

"And there was one other thing that would have been of great significance to William the publican. Thomas and William, the two brothers who ran Woolmers and Brickendon in Van Diemen's Land, had around a hundred convicts between them as their workforce. They shared them as work required on each estate. Who knows what my William thought about this? He had been a convict while the other Archers ran a convict workforce."

"I imagine that would have spurred him on to prove himself and to repudiate the past," said Lilian.

"Although, I also discovered that the Archers in Tasmania were strong supporters of the Anti-Transportation League in the 1850s. People are complicated, aren't they?"

"They are. So, what did you think when you visited the estates? You did see both?"

"Yes, I did. Both of them were quite an experience, but they were quite different to each other."

"Is this a square or two in the quilt?"

"Yes."

* * * * *

I went to Woolmers Estate, which is now in the hands of the Woolmer Foundation, there being no more descendants of the Archer family. The last person was called Thomas Archer, the sixth direct descendant of the Thomas Archer who was the first Archer to come to Van Diemen's Land in about 1813. The last Archer was an only child, and he never married. He died in 1994, in his fifties. His seemed to have had a sad, disconnected life. He spent much of his time at home, and even then, in just a small part of the house.

I went on a tour of the house with a guide, and Thomas's living quarters look like the rooms of a child, with children's toys prominent. He never seemed to have established a connection with the wider world, or even his own property, the one that had been in his family for about 180 years. It was disturbing. The guide explained Thomas the Sixth in terms of his mother, who kept him sheltered from contact with the world.

His father, Thomas Edward Cathcart Archer (1892–1975), became an orchardist, and grew apples on the property for distribution locally and on the mainland. In the 20th century, apples certainly became a signature crop in Tasmania. It was "the Apple Isle".

The orchard utilised only a small portion of the estate. When I walked around the property, I was walking among a succession of buildings dating from the very first years right up to the late twentieth century.

When I looked into the various buildings, it was like looking at snapshots of different stages of its life. There was a chapel that dated from the years when convicts worked here and attended church on Sundays. Thomas the orchardist had repurposed the chapel as his apple sorting shed. The sorting and packing equipment was still there in the building, and some boxes had "T. Archer, Longford" stencilled on them.

The Thomas who came before the orchardist, Thomas Cathcart Archer (1862-1934), had had little interest in farming. He leased out the farmland and took up sports and leisure. He was a good-enough golfer to have played in the Australian Open. The disconnection between the land and the male of the line came in the generation before. Thomas William Chalmers Archer (1840–1890) had come into his inheritance at the age of ten, when his father died of scarlet fever at the age of twenty-six. The land was leased out for the first time, and the boy was sent to England to be educated.

However, when the son returned as a young man he did not take up farming. The land continued to be leased out. This set the pattern for the subsequent generations.

The foundation that now runs the estate has restored many of the buildings and their furnishings for viewing by the public. The formal gardens, probably about two hectares, are well-tended. There are many hedges and flower beds, and roses feature prominently. The grounds are populated with many buildings, from the new Nigel Peck Centre, which is the reception area, museum and restaurant, to the main house and the farm buildings, going right back to the 1820s.

The house was built and then added to, with greater grandeur, as Thomas Archer sought to demonstrate his success. Many of the furnishings were ordered from England. There are some oddities. A large framed mirror was ordered to go over the fireplace in the ladies' retiring room, but when it arrived it was too large for the space. The solution was to install it on the opposite wall, for which purpose a window had to be blocked out. From the inside this is perfectly fine, but from the outside it doesn't make sense that one of the several domed windows is not a window.

The first Thomas spent the last twenty years of his life bed-ridden. He had the room set up as a permanent abode. When he died, they had to cut a wider section out of the wall so they could get his body out, he was so big.

The Archers of Woolmers in the twentieth century lived off the wealth of the land, travelling the world and participating in sports like tennis, golf and yachting. In the end, this line of the family died out, leaving the estate falling into ruin. The foundation set about restoring the property and caring for it as a tourist destination showcasing a major farming property of Tasmania's past.

All of this is history, and it is history at a distance from me. The divergence between this branch of the Archer family and mine occurred long ago, around 1800. So I am suitably dispassionate about hearing an account of this family, especially in its domestic details. I noted oddities like the little curtains on stands in the ladies' retiring room. Obligingly, the guide pointed out that the purpose of these artefacts was to protect the delicate skin of the ladies from the direct heat of the fire.

One of the wives liked pink, and she liked redecorating the house. Much of the surviving décor is due to her. She married into the family; she was from Launceston. She was considered to be beautiful, and she was known as the Duchess of Launceston. I wondered if this was the source of my mother's idea that the Archers in Tasmania were lords or earls, that they held some kind of title, but the reality was, there were plenty of reasons to draw on.

There was one thing that struck me more than anything else during the tour of the house. There was a cupboard full of medicines and toiletries. It seemed to date mostly from around the 1930s, and included an emergency sheet of instructions for if someone was bitten by a snake. (Of course, today, the instructions are not considered to be helpful.) The thing that struck me was a container of Johnson's baby powder in among the very dated medical and cosmetic supplies. My mother had used Johnson's baby powder all her life after having a shower, right up to her last days (she was 93 when she died). No changes in contemporary beliefs, customs or advertising had ever changed this practice.

Seeing it there was as if my mother had a direct connection to these Archers, despite the 200 years of separation between this branch of the family and ours. What gave it all the more impact was that the container looked new, although all the other items were from the original time. It was as if the original item had gone astray, but the person looking after the collection knew its importance to the user, and so had substituted a modern container instead.

Later, I talked to the tour guide again, and told her my connection to the Archers. However, she was not family, she was simply employed as a guide, so she was coming from a distance, from a place of having no connection except general interest and professional knowledge.

I can understand it in terms of longings that abide in families across generations. I think in this case it was the perspective of the privileged class in contrast to servants. My mother saw herself as servant class - honourable, loyal and skilled. She would have liked to have had someone to serve who was worthy. But in her lifetime, that paradigm evaporated, and it only survives in pockets. It even disappeared in the Tasmanian branch of the Archer family.

They had servants, because there were several people on whom the servants had to wait; there was system of bells on wires that went to the servants' quarters. Each of the bells made a different sound, so the servants would know who it was that needed their attention.

The tour guide had told us that, as the family contracted over the years, the woman who looked after the household began to take household items and sell them off. Unfortunately, this stratagem was doomed to failure, as the items she took had the family crest on them, so it was obvious around the district where they had come from. The woman was dismissed from service.

It was clear that William Archer, my mother's great grandfather, had no wish to be anyone's servant, but I suspect he liked the paradigm of master-servant, and would have enjoyed receiving the service of others. Thus, the paradigm continues. I watched the prevalence of this paradigm while I was growing up. I have no wish to serve others, and no wish to have servants of my own. This is my legacy for the next generation.

Square 20

"Interesting," said Lilian. "I wasn't expecting that."

"It was an interesting visit," I replied. "I wasn't expecting what I found. It's different when you have a connection, no matter how remote it is. Then it's no longer textbook history, it's somehow personal, as if the things that happened and the decisions that people made with their lives matter. Their decisions could have been different, and the outcomes could have been different."

"True, but there is the whole momentum of history to be taken into account too. It was a farm during the convict era, and then there was the growth of the colony, then there was Federation and a war, and then the Depression, and in that context this was one little family, not entirely in charge of its fate."

"They collected things, you know," I said. They didn't pass them on when life changed. For example, I went into a stable, and it still had all the horse equipment hanging on the walls, and standing next to it were two generations of motor cars, one from 1910 and one from the 1930s. It was as if they were collecting souvenirs from stages in history. In another building there was a Chrysler from the 1950s."

"Perhaps it's ironic," said Lilian. "For a long time, all those things gathered dust and rust. Now, they are a great asset, to give people today a window into the past. It's priceless."

"It was certainly that. The place still has a spirit about it from days gone by. I walked around and walked through different periods of time. The baker's house is still there, from the 1820s, and the blacksmith's shop. There is a huge shed from the heyday of wool, for shearing sheep and sorting and packing wool. There are servants' quarters. There are rows of machinery still intact, horse-drawn and tractor-drawn. It must have been like a whole village for quite a while."

"You sound excited."

"It was dazzling, like stepping into a picture. And then, near the main house, there is a path that goes down to the river. There was a punt in the old days, to ferry people and goods across. Often the convicts would have to walk from one farm to the other – Brickendon – at the beginning and end of the day, about three or four miles. The landscape is the same today, with the hills in the distance beyond the fields."

"I take it that the farm was successful in the early days?"

"It was. The crops grew, the sheep were merinos and produced excellent wool, and everything was in demand. Wealth followed."

"On the backs of convict labour."

"But the Archer brothers were supporters of the anti-transportation movement. Do you think they changed their views?"

"You could suspect that they were opportunists. Convict labour had served them well, but maybe they could see that it was no longer best for the economy. Maybe they saw that convicts would no longer work willingly, and force would not achieve results in the longer term. But maybe all of those years of having convicts led to some learning, and it was not just about economics. In the end, maybe morality and 'what works' turn out to be the same thing."

"It seldom seems to be the case," sighed Lilian, "but maybe the wheel that is turning is just slow. Maybe we get there in the end. How is the quilt shaping up?"

"There are more elements. There is Brickendon, for a start. I told you it was different."

"Okay. Tell me."

* * * * *

I went to Brickendon. I was told it was still a working farm, and it was still being run by the Archer family; they have been running it continuously since the 1820s. Thomas Archer had been the first one to come to Van Diemen's Land, and he settled at Woolmers. His brother Joseph followed in 1821, and he established the farm called Panshanger. William came in 1824, and he was the one who established Brickendon. The fourth brother to come to the colony was Edward, who settled at Leverington.

The father, William Archer, eventually joined his sons in 1827, at first settling at Woolmers before acquiring other properties of his own. However, he did not live long in the colony. He was killed in a fall from a horse in January 1833, although, let it be said, he was close to eighty years old.

William Archer, who was the oldest of the sons, carried on at Brickendon, as did his brothers on their properties on the Norfolk Plains. They created a landscape that was similar to the one in which they had grown up, clearing the native vegetation and introducing new grasses. All the names of their properties come from the names of estates in Hertford.

Brickendon was a mixed enterprise, with cropping on the lower ground near the Macquarie River and sheep and cattle raising for both wool and meat production on the higher lands. William had brought out thirty merino sheep with him from England to start his flocks.

Both William of Brickendon and Thomas of Woolmers went into public life, as members of the Legislative Council in Tasmania, and in other roles such as magistrate, justice of the peace and councillor on the local council. The Archer name has a reputation in Tasmania for both innovative farming methods and for service in public life.

At Brickendon, the name William has been passed down, and the current family still lives in the original homestead.

When I arrived at the car park, there was a school bus that had just arrived, and a young lady was standing nearby, holding a young dog to stop it from being too enthusiastic and jumping all over the children as they emerged from the bus. She was clearly from the property and was the designated guide for the school's visit. She wore jeans comfortably and her presence was amiable and selflessly confident.

The children were about six years old and were as excited as the dog. When they had all assembled, with their teachers, the guide led them inside the gate.

She knew exactly where to start, with the ducklings and lambs. Soon, all the children were gathered around the animals and making that quiet but excited buzz of noise. When she had a moment, she greeted me. Rather than leading me to the ducklings and lambs, she gave me a large map of the property and invited me to explore it all. She also recommended, if I was interested in the history of the place, to sit down and watch a show on a television set that was about the history of the family.

It was an appropriate recommendation. I had plenty of time, so I sat and watched the whole show. It was called 'Dynasty', and it was a fitting title. I had established that the current generation is the sixth one from the original William Archer who settled at Brickendon. It also seems fitting that he was born in 1788, the year the Australian colony was founded.

With my modest background, I wondered how I would regard the Archers of Brickendon. They began in privilege, with grants of thousands of acres of land from the governor, and they had a workforce of convicts, an example of how the poor continually gave to the rich. And yet, the values of hard work, decency and innovation seemed to seep through the generations at Brickendon. There was a story on the 'Dynasty' show that was an indicator.

During the convict days, when convicts had served out their sentence at the farm, many of them stayed, and were kept on as farm labourers. I compared that with Edward and Sarah Lewis, who just wanted to get away, and were also encouraged to go away, after their sentences had expired. But at Brickendon, in one case, the convict still had a wife back in Ireland, and it was the solicitations of William Archer with the authorities in Ireland that led to the convict's wife coming to join her husband in Tasmania. That was unabashed evidence of humanity, of care that went well beyond mere economic management of land and workers. It spoke of relationship. It is relationship that enables things to endure.

I looked at all the buildings and took lots of photos. Not far from the main building is the first modest hut that William Archer lived in – just two rooms and a fireplace. And around it are buildings that cover all the time since then. It is like a small village. It has a cookhouse, a blacksmith's workshop, a formidable building that was for grain storage, a shearing shed with fresh wool strewn about on the sorting tables, and a small but lovely chapel.

When I went back to the reception building, the lady guide told me that she was the latest in the Archer line, and that she had been in the 'Dynasty' show, but she had only been a girl then. I told her that we had a connection, if you go back eight generations and to Hertfordshire. I told her that my mother's father's name was Thomas Richard Archer; the names 'Thomas' and 'Richard' had appeared often in the 'Dynasty' show. She smiled broadly, seemingly delighted to discover a new connection that confirmed faith in family.

I went across to the other side of the road to see the gardens around the house, the house the family still lives in. When I parked, a lady came out of the house to get into her car, and she gave me a happy smile, no defensiveness or looking at you as if you were merely a voyeur or a customer. I spent some time looking around the gardens. They are very English, and everything was in flower at the time, so it was especially beautiful.

What struck me, walking around the gardens and thinking about this quite separate family, connected to me at the last back in the early 1800s, wasn't just the difference between having wealth and not having it, but the very idea of having a known past. The young Archer lady seemed to have an easy relationship with her past. She showed me a big book they had sitting on the counter which was on the history of the Archers in Tasmania – one of Neil Chick's books – and she seemed at peace with the past and happy to see herself as a continuation of it.

In contrast, what I had was the partly fabricated past my mother had been given and that she passed onto me in good faith, and on my father's side, nothing. I had had to dig for the knowledge alone, for example, finding out about the lives of Edward and Sarah Lewis. I have uncovered stories of sadness and of great achievement among all my ancestors, and many stories of the fearful voyages from Cornwall, Scotland and England to Australia to start a new life.

Of course, it is all fine, and the discoveries have been exciting, they have created a huge vista where before, all I had was a blank canvas that many people said I should ignore.

When I was growing up, we were encouraged to think of ourselves as a new generation without a past. The past, such as it was in my parents' experience, could be dispensed with; it was merely a platform from which to project us into the future. We would go on to do great things, have better jobs and better houses. I even think my parents' generation were utopians. After the horrors of two world wars and the Great Depression, I think they were tempted to believe that the modern world was bringing us all into a utopian vision.

I blame advertising.

It was a mistake of my parents to think the past was dispensable. It clearly has an effect on us. Walking around the Brickendon gardens, I appreciated that many of the plants and trees here went back to the early 1800s. We live in a society that believes it can fake time. A mature garden can be produced in a month if you have enough money; you just bring in mature trees using a crane. But I don't believe in it, because it reinforces the idea that you can get rid of it just as quickly. I want time, slow time, the time it takes to grow things for real.

I think my mother realised eventually that the past was irrevocable; you couldn't take it away, and also, that ultimately, it couldn't hurt you. After I started exploring the family history, she even gave me the occasional word of encouragement. One time she sent me a note that said, "Keep looking. You never know what you will find." Did she mean, maybe I would find a convict? I don't think she had thought it through that far, but it was an intriguing message.

The other thought that came while I was walking around the Brickendon garden, so much more intimate than the Woolmer Estate gardens, was the difference between the pasts of the two Archer families involved. It was almost a morality tale – one family lives high on the wealth and distances itself from the farm, and then the family dies out and the property is now a showcase run for tourists by a foundation; the other family is still alive, and the farm has been running continuously for nearly two hundred years as an active, profitable farm. Side by side, it is quite extraordinary.

It is also instructive to look at the histories of these two Archer families against my mother's Archer family. The Duke of Edinburgh Hotel was William the convict's grand gesture in his adopted homeland, and the hotel remained in the family for around a hundred years, but my mother's father seems to have been a fringe dweller in the family. He made his living as a trade painter. He was a businessman too – he had his own painting business, but mum said he went broke in the Depression, and he died before he was fifty. I suspect that failure did not go down well in the Archer clan.

Family history brings its challenges. It can be something you have to live up to, or something you have to live down.

Square 21

I sent this piece to Lilian. Later, I rang her.

"Yes, I liked it," she said. "I find it funny that even when you try to be a current-day tourist, you end up looking at the past, and not even the past generally, but your own family's past."

"Blame my mother," I replied. "She didn't have to say anything about the Tasmanian Archers."

"Well, I suppose you've realised at a family level what Tasmania has realised as a state, that every present has a past, and there is something to be learned by admitting the past."

"True, not that I get any sense of how you are supposed to feel about all the things that you see. For example, the original Thomas Archer has an illness and spends the last twenty years of his life in bed. When he dies, they have to cut a hole in the wall to get him out. What are we supposed to think about that? Or the cars pile up in stables and sheds over a period of fifty years. What are we supposed to think about that? Why did these things happen, and why did they happen that way? Whose motivations or attitudes or capacities are on display?"

"There are some clues, I am sure," responded Lilian. You've mentioned some yourself, and in any case, you can't know everything. It is the past, you know. I think there is a place for this square in your quilt."

"I wonder if there are anchor points in the past, like, a key person whose shadow casts down over the succeeding generations. The William Archer whose sons came to Tasmania seems to be an anchor point. His ambition triggered a mass migration to Tasmania, and the effects of this are still evident today, far beyond the family itself. I think my William Archer's ambition parallels that, leading to the establishment of the hotel in Sydney. He certainly affected the subsequent generations of his family."

"But we must be affected by all our ancestors, mustn't we?"

"Yes, but the anchor points are the people who had a big impact on the trail of the whole family. I think what you are talking about is at a more personal level. I would call them touch points. This could be about preferences, like both enjoying gardening, or having a knack for technical skills."

"Or enjoying living?" Lilian was calling me back to earth.

"Yes. And maybe family history can make you aware of what is not there, and it's up to you to not make the same mistakes."

"But you can draw on any strengths that you see."

"Yes, I can; and we can."

"Where to now?"

"I've been wondering about Aborigines."

"So far, you haven't mentioned them."

"I know. That's because they haven't turned up."

"But they were there in Tasmania before white people came."

"Yes, and I saw stories about them while I was in Tasmania."

93

"Tell me."

* * * * *

"Aborigines are nomads; they are always moving around, they kill wildlife for food, and they build bark lean-tos for shelter." That was my received picture of Aborigines, from school. In later life, not much had changed in this picture. But I have been reading Bruce Pascoe's book, *Dark Emu*, and he makes a strong case for a more complex picture of Aboriginal life This is particularly true in Tasmania, because it is colder there.

I went to the museum in Launceston (there are two; this was the one in the city). It had an exhibition of Aboriginal life. It showed me, for the first time, a model of a permanent aboriginal dwelling – a stick frame covered with grasses and a mud covering over that. When the weather is colder, it makes more sense to stay in one place and make warmer living quarters. This is a phase shift in my understanding of Aboriginal life. Across the continent of Australia, the different living conditions led to different lifestyles, adapted to place.

Many years ago, I wrote the history of a shire in northern New South Wales. In it I included a brief account of the Aborigines, limited by the brief amount of time I had for research. I was also frustrated by the limited amount of information I found out about their food. A study by an academic concluded that they lived mainly on meat – kangaroo and wallaby, goanna, possum, echidna and so on. Also, fish when they were available. There was scant reference to vegetables, grains and fruit, and I just didn't believe that, but that's all I managed to find out at the time.

The exhibition at Launceston showed that the Aborigines of this area ate a wide range of foods, not just meats, but also plants – grains, vegetables and fruits! It also emphasised the importance of seafood in their diet, including shellfish. Suddenly, things felt right, after all this time. It was also apparent that their cooking methods were far more complex than simply throwing a piece of meat on the fire like it was a good old Australian barbecue.

All of the Aboriginal items in the exhibition were appropriate and adequate for their purpose. For example, there were canoes,

94

because fishing was important, and there were substantial nets for catching fish. These tools served them for countless generations.

I contrast this with fridges. When I was a child, our family had an ice chest to keep things cool. The ice man used to have to come every couple of days with a new block of ice. It was not a very efficient way to keep things cool. Refrigerators were much better. But at this point, my mother was satisfied. She said she did not need fridges to keep on 'improving'. I don't think she meant this rigidly; fridges have improved and she recognised this.

I think the distinction she was making was about frivolous and gratuitous changes that were promoted as improvements. If it's better it's better, but only if it's not encumbered by an ideology that says things are always and inevitably getting better. I think that's the difference between our society and traditional Aboriginal society – they knew when something was appropriate and adequate for the purpose. They didn't have an advertising industry.

Looking at everything in the exhibition, I could see that every aspect of life had been considered, and appropriate, elegant solutions had been devised. In my childhood perception, it was hard to say what Aboriginal people did with their time, other than that the men hunted wallabies. Looking at all the articles on show, it was easy to see that Aborigines lived a rich life, that they made a wide variety of artefacts for practical and ceremonial purposes, and spent much of their time engaging in this common life. From this, it was not a great leap to think about their culture, and their laws and worldview that made life whole.

I know that the relationship between the Aborigines of Tasmania and the colonists from Britain was brutal, exacerbated by the fact that the colony itself, as a convict settlement, was brutal. The colony had not been established on the basis that people already possessed the land and would be unwilling to give it up, would not even have a concept of what "giving up their land" might mean. It was always going to be ugly.

The only contextual factor is that similar scenarios had been enacted around the world over a period of about three hundred years, by a host of European nations – in America, South America, Asia and Africa. But if we are going to admit that, we also need to acknowledge that invasions and conquests have occurred for thousands of years, without any pretence of international law to moderate them. The British Isles themselves suffered a succession of invasions. But it was the conceit that Britain was bringing civilisation to the world that made the Tasmanian situation worse, because of its hypocrisy.

And here we all are, the de facto benefactors of an invasion. A war was declared in Van Diemen's Land in the mid-1820s against the blacks. It lasted until around 1830, and it included the formation of a rag-tag army to sweep the entire island to round up the blacks. The army, made up of all-sorts, free settlers and ex-convicts as well as real soldiers, was given a uniform to make it clear that this was a legitimate initiative of the government.

Women from Cascades Female Factory were among those who made the uniforms. Not Sarah; she didn't arrive until 1850. So much history had already happened before she arrived. One supposes that she found out through the chain of gossip exchanged among female convicts.

There is some comfort, although very small comfort it is, in the fact that there were some voices in the British colony of the time who recognised the impossibility of the situation, that the Aborigines lived here and had every right to continue to do so. It was fundamentally incompatible with the convict settlement. The academic Henry Reynolds has done a wonderful job of finding these voices and presenting them.

The most tortured voice of all would have to be that of George Robinson, a builder by trade and an untrained preacher, who became the official conciliator with the Aborigines. He devised the 'solution' of persuading Aborigines to relocate to Flinders Island, off the north coast of Tasmania, where they would be able to live their traditional life. It was a 'lesser of two evils' solution.

Only a small number of Aborigines took up the offer, and the island became a miserable prison rather than a nirvana. Many of the Aborigines wasted away and died. Robinson later became the official Protector of Aborigines in Victoria, despite the fact that his mission in Tasmania had failed.

It was Captain Cook who articulated the essential insight into the Aborigines, going right back to his voyage of discovery in 1770. He observed that there was nothing the Aborigines wanted from them, they, the grand lords of what was to become "the greatest empire the world has ever known". Nothing that Cook tried to entice them with was perceived to be of any value in their world. Of course, after settlement, things like steel axes, and the meat of sheep, were perceived to be of value, but there was ultimately a high price to pay for that.

I learned another story. When I went on a three-day walk in the northwest of Tasmania, in the Tarkine area, I learned that Aboriginal women used to dive for abalone. They would smear their bodies with seal fat to protect themselves from the cold, and dive. White men who were in the northwest to kill seals and whales would kidnap these women, both for their diving prowess and for sex. Accordingly, there were children produced from these relationships who carried Aboriginal blood and knew Aboriginal culture. This kills the tidy conception that Truganini was the last Tasmanian Aborigine.

There is a lot in the past that is difficult to come to terms with, and the further you go back, the more it opens up. There are sins and transgressions, and there are angry voices who call for recompense. I want my recompense too. I want to know why Constable John Smith found it necessary to demand that Sarah Crosby 'move on' on 31st January 1849 in London outside the Refuge for the Houseless Poor. Where is my satisfaction? Can I demand it from his descendants?

On the other hand, do I want a blanket exemption from generational accountability? That would be to suggest there is no accountability for wrongs done in the past. At the same time, there is an absurdity about demanding that the Vikings apologise for invading England. There are no longer Vikings, and England is no longer what it was then either. Any apology would be a fiction on both sides.

If I were to suggest what it looks like to reconcile with the past, I have already suggested that one of my ancestors had a grievance that had a significant impact on her subsequent life – Sarah Crosby. The next step would be to say that the incident was not simply personal, like two people having a fight; it was systemic. I would maintain that Sarah was Irish, and the Irish were hated in London at that time. So far, my case looks good, it looks like a possible class action suit.

Then, my opponent might argue that the outcome for Sarah was probably much better than it might otherwise have been, so any damages awarded would be minimal. She ended up having a new life, marrying and having children, living in Sydney and having her life acknowledged with an impressive gravestone in Rookwood cemetery. Left in London, she probably would have died of starvation and cold before the winter was over.

My opponent would continue, that Constable John Smith is long dead, and he should not be pursued beyond the grave. I respond that this is a systemic issue; it is not just John Smith personally. The English society has to answer for its hatred of the Irish, and the harm that that caused for Sarah personally. I ask them to explain the scar on her left cheek. This is the crux of my argument.

My opponent is adamant: there is no case to answer. That was then, this is now. Put it behind you.

But I feel the hatred of the policeman that incited Sarah's act of desperation. She felt it, and that's why she was desperate. These people would be happy to see her dead. It is wrong, and it is heart-breaking. She is just a young girl, cold, starving, without parents, and homeless, a long way from home.

The thing is, there is no solution legally. A win would not be a win, it would be empty and meaningless. In your angry moments, you want someone to pay, but there is no one, even though it was wrong. They are not there anymore. But Sarah is. She is in the carving on the stone, with her final statement – I lived, and I am a native of Waterford, Ireland! And you have to thank her daughter for granting her that statement, for recognising its importance. And I thank her daughter too.

It is this life we have to weave, not the past, but it behoves us well to recognise what happened in the past, as near as we can understand it. I am sorry for history; I am sorry that it happened. I can only say that I am here nevertheless. We are all here nevertheless. The biggest crimes I can see are invasion and conquest. I am asking for a future that turns thousands of years of history around.

I talk about Sarah, but I think also about Aborigines who were killed or collected up and deposited on a convenient island, a long way out of sight. Even the English who could be described generously as confused but well-intentioned did no good, because they never saw or felt the Aboriginal mind. Not that it would have been difficult; there were a few of the English who could see the obvious – a people that were fellow humans, a people who lived here and had lived here for ages past, and had the right to call this place home.

One accepts that we are here, and we cannot go back and change what happened. But how is it that we know we would never behave like that again? Is there anything about us that assures us we would not demonise the poor, and blacks, that we would not take people, who were simply desperate to live, away from their homeland to a rabble prison a world away, never to return? And steal another people's lands in the process? And declare war on them? And enslave our own, and flog them for discipline, and tear the skin off their backs? And lock them in dark coffins without light or voice?

What is it that assures us of our humanity in this day?

Square 22

If the world is difficult, there are places we can retreat to. If there are larrikins, there are also bastions of convention. I found a bastion of convention at the other Launceston museum, the one on the outskirts of town, over the River Esk. This was the museum at what used to be the tram depot. There was even a tram there. I suppose I shouldn't have been surprised, but the tram was actually the first thing I saw. I was walking from a distance, walking along the old tram track. There used to be trams in Launceston! This one said it was going to Newstead via Elphin Road.

The tram looked very fetching. It had been restored. The wooden panelling, the wooden seats, all had been painted with the shiniest of paint, and the windows all sparkled, they were so clean. I got close and was taking a photo when suddenly the tram moved off. I wasn't expecting that. Then I noticed that the tram had a little motorised trolley behind it, and two men were driving this little trolley, which was dragging the tram along.

I suppose trams were part of the modern dream of utopia. They were quaint, they were public, so they were available to all, and they celebrated electricity. Could things get any better than this? And did they have to, anyway? Surely not.

The museum was not huge, but it was full of unexpected things. Although, on reflection, isn't that what we expect of museums? In one section it had skeletons of dinosaurs, and a skeleton of a giant wombat, different to the diprotodon; this one was called a *zygomaturus tasmanica*. It was wombat-shaped and about two metres long. It died out about 45,000 years ago. I imagined it with a saddle and me riding it!

There were also geological exhibits, including dolerite rocks that I had seen at Bruny Island. Now I knew how to spell the word properly.

The temporary exhibition was where I found a bastion of convention. The exhibition was for a famous Australian housewife of the 1950s, Marjorie Bligh, who wrote many books for the benefit of housewives. She was billed as "The domestic goddess". I think I had heard of her when I was a child. Perhaps there had been an article about her in the *Women's Weekly*, which my mother used to buy.

Marjorie had lived near Launceston, hence the exhibition. She wrote all her books with a biro, and the pictures were drawn or pasted into a scrapbook. Then she would approach a publisher to go about the publishing process. Some of the scrapbooks on display were about cooking creatively, making your home beautiful, and making interesting things out of commonly available materials. They were things that we would now cringe at. I think this was where the crocheted toilet roll holder came from.

Marjorie was said to be a hard worker, a very determined woman, and a great exponent of self-publicity. The exhibition was presented with a nice show of balance. It was neither sycophantic nor demeaning. It was a depiction of a bygone era, with all its quaintness, innocence and foibles. There was sad irony in it as well. For all that Marjorie was billed as the domestic goddess, her married life was not all a bed of roses.

Her first husband was a serious man, and prone to violence against her, and they ended up getting divorced. Her second husband seemed to be a better match, but he died, and there was a third husband. The perfect life is hard to concoct. One of the signs in the exhibition commented, "Marjorie's marriages demonstrate the conflict between her religious beliefs and her romantic ideals of marriage." However, I would have thought that her religious ideals and her romantic notions were pretty much in alignment. The problem was more the refusal of reality to align with those notions.

There were lots of posters which were Marjorie's own posters from her time of fame. One shows her taking a tray of perfect scones out of an old-fashioned oven (today we would say, new ovens are much better). Another poster presented "Marjorie Bligh's Bonza Happy Home Recipe": "4 cups of love, 2 cups of loyalty, 3 cups of forgiveness, 1 cup of friendship, 5 spoons of hope, 2 spoons of tenderness, 4 litres of faith, 1 barrel of laughter." This was followed by instructions for making the happy home: "Take love and loyalty, mix it thoroughly with faith.... Bake it with sunshine, Serve daily with generous helpings."

Fine sentiments, but when times are tough, sentiments like this tend to be trite and lacking in nourishment, and one feels the need for some grit. Yet Marjorie must have been endowed with some of this grit, for she bounced back from her marital setbacks and continued to produce her popular books. I liked the awkward nod in this poster to the metric age (4 litres of faith).

So, Marjorie Bligh, flawed but determined bastion of convention, when women's domestic role was a central plank of post-war utopianism. From this feminine extreme, I went to see the masculine extreme, a blacksmith's workshop, which had been used to carry out maintenance for the trams. The huge space had been left intact and there was a soft layer of dust over all the tools, benches and machines. It was eerie and magnificent. You could walk in among huge machines and view lots of small areas where specific tasks were carried out – welding, folding steel sheets, cutting lengths of steel, and blacksmithing. Those days, too, are mostly gone.

I remembered some words of Lilian's: "I'm not going to tell you it's a better world. It's shinier, and there's more concrete and glass."

* * * * *

The museum also contained a large exhibit that dealt with something I was quite unfamiliar with, a ship called the *Sydney Cove*. It came from Calcutta in India. It was an existing ship but was renamed for the journey. Some entrepreneurs had heard about the new convict colony in Sydney, and thought it was a great opportunity for supplying goods to a new market. The year was 1796. The ship was packed with all sorts of goods.

The *Sydney Cove* made it all the way across the Indian Ocean and across to the east coast of Australia, but it suffered serious damage in storms. It foundered just north of Tasmania. The ship was wrecked near the shore of an island, which is now named after the episode, as Preservation Island. The captain and sailors got to shore, and managed to bring ashore most of the goods the ship was carrying. The captain was clearly a cautious man, and the alcohol was taken to a different island nearby.

Somehow they needed to get to the real Sydney Cove. A party in a longboat set off for Sydney, across Bass Strait and up the east coast. The others stayed on the island. The saga continued when the longboat was wrecked off the coast of Victoria. The survivors ended up making it to Sydney on foot, having some tense encounters with Aboriginal groups along the way. The Governor of the colony sent a boat down to the island and, over several months, much of the cargo and the sailors from the island were brought back to Sydney. An extraordinary tale!

This adventure (or misadventure) is also the source of a story about bottles of beer that were recovered from the shipwreck. The bottles were sealed with wax, so they survived time and being submerged in sea water, and the yeast was extracted and used to make new beer, not only unique but also saleable, over two hundred years later.

I was thinking along these lines – old worlds, new worlds – and who is to say what's better and what's worse, when I came back to the evening in December 1973 after I had toured Port Arthur. I had met up with some of the people I knew, and we were having a drink at a hotel. We had been discussing the morality of the convict system. I forgot about the rest of that evening.

* * * * *

The local dance at Port Arthur (29 December 1973)

I was just sitting with my drink, thinking about this. I was glad when Ute and Matina suggested we go to a local dance. It was a proper dance, a dress-up event in the local hall, a Tasmanian up-country frolic billed as an Evening Spectacular.

The local dance. The mothers were all there, their daughters dancing under supervision. The men talked out the back. The boys were all smartly dressed, unlike our more casual attire, but they tolerated our presence amiably enough. The band sported an organist, a pianist and a drummer. Perhaps we wanted to feel a part of it too. In the progressive dances we progressed, and went around the hall that way, having met half the locals by the time we finished. We all wore smiles, happy ones.

After the dance was over, the four of us went carousing down at the beach, a jaunt which involved singing and laughing with gay abandon, and dancing about frivolously. And I was enjoying the renewed use of all my limbs after the ordeals of this year.

Sunday 30 December

I made my way back to Hobart, in preparation for flying back to Sydney. I travelled up to Mount Wellington, and the shadow of it over the city proved to me that it was still just a country town. Up there the wind was blowing fiercely, with ice in its talons. The rocks made a moonscape – bleak, broken, scattered. And all down the slopes were not trees but ghosts of trees from the 1967 bushfires, horrified spectres without life. What small bushes there were clung tightly in the clefts of rocks for life.

Square 23

"History can be hard," said Lilian. "It is not all exploits and heroism. It's no wonder people look for comforts and small joys. We have a hard time with the ghosts."

"Unfortunately," I said, "it has become an argument about wallowing in emotionalism. It is as if emotions are completely detached from the rest of our lives. In the grand days of Woolmer, the wealthy would get together and have dinners and leisure events, with polo and extravagant cuisine, smoking, port and whisky for the men in the den, piano for the ladies in the retiring room. These were self-perpetuating affairs, where refinement was continually taken to new heights.

"I think that emotions are being treated like that, as if they have become a recreational pursuit with no anchor in real life. They lead to their own hysteria. But what if we go back to real events, and consider what emotions belong to those events? Surely it is appropriate to be upset about men being flogged, and black people being killed for daring to live on their own land?"

"Perhaps that is why so many people don't want to talk about the past," said Lilian. "They say, 'We need to put it behind us.'"

I laughed. "Those people have got so much behind them, they live their lives in the shadows of demons and ghosts. Oddly, when I went to New Norfolk, where the mental asylum and other institutions used to be, there was an advertisement for ghost tours at night."

"Do you think people believe in ghosts or demons?"

"The demons and ghosts are simply all the things we have 'put behind us' without resolving them or making peace with them."

"Maybe these people can't see any way of resolving what's in the past," Lilian suggested. "Maybe they are afraid they will fall into a cauldron of emotion and drown. Maybe they think their whole life will collapse or be taken from them."

"I have a question," Lilian continued. "For something to be a square in this quilt you are making, does it have to be resolved? For example, if you take Marjorie Bligh, is there an agreed attitude now towards her and her 'domestic goddess' books? What if you apply this perspective to your encounters?"

"Mmm. Marjorie Bligh was a phenomenon of her time and her books were bought by a lot of women, who presumably read them and carried out some of the projects. They were doing something to help create domestic bliss in their own lives. Later, that vision started to break up. That's what happens over time; things fall apart or evolve into something else. In the same way, I have experienced things and had ideas about them. The further I go, the more things seem to be part of a bigger picture. It's not resolved, but something is taking shape."

"Ah," said Lilian, "does it all fit together, then?"

"I think that the bigger the picture, the more things fit."

"What is next?"

"I don't think it's a square; it is just a thread. I found a reference in the family history of Thomas Archer of Woolmers about Aborigines."

"I remember you said Thomas Archer first took up the Woolmers land very early in the history of the colony."

"Yes, it was 1817, so one thinks there had to have been Aborigines around the district at that time. Anyway, remember that Thomas Archer had initially been in Sydney in a government role? While he was there, he also met the lady that he married."

"Oh?"

"Her name was Susannah Hortle. She was the daughter of a soldier in the New South Wales Corp, James Hortle. He had come to the Port Jackson colony in 1791 as a soldier on the *Salamander*. Thomas married Susannah in December 1816 in Launceston. But earlier, James Hortle had been to Van Diemen's Land as part of a party to establish a settlement in the north of the island. It was not long after Bass and flinders had explored the area. There were a couple of attempted settlements, on either side of the Tamar River, at George Town and at Yorktown, dating from 1804.

"James Hortle was speared to death by Aborigines near George Town on 25 June 1808. He is buried in "The Soldier's Grave" at Yorktown, on the western side of the Tamar River. That's all I know. I don't know the circumstances. Did Hortle cause an affront to the Aborigines? At the least, it indicates that the relationships between the whites and the blacks were not amicable."

"Yes, that is a thread," Lilian agreed.

* * * * *

I went to George Town. It is the town near the mouth of the Tamar River. Yes, this was where Private James Hortle, Thomas Archer's father-in-law, was stationed in 1808, and where he met his death.

Near the town there is a sheltered bay where about twenty boats and sailing boats were moored. In a park there were some tall wooden statues of men, who included the explorers George Bass and Matthew Flinders. The statues had been carved with a chain saw by a local artist. There were very good.

After that, I found a museum dedicated to Bass and Flinders. An older lady was at reception, and she talked about the boats on show and the lives and exploits of Bass and Flinders. Then I walked around slowly. There were many boats in the building; it had once been a cinema. Most of the boats were hung from the ceiling, but the main one, the *Norfolk*, was on the floor with the tip of the mast almost brushing up against the high corrugated iron roof.

It was a replica, made by a talented enthusiast with a group of helpers about twenty years ago. When it was finished, the roof was taken off the cinema and the boat was lowered in by a crane, and the roof was put back on. It had a mast and sail, and it was about forty feet high.

A lot of the voyages of Bass and Flinders were made in the *Norfolk*. The *Investigator* was the boat they used to circumnavigate Australia. There was also a small boat called the *Tom Thumb*. And a model of a cat called Trim, who survived a few storms and one overboard episode. The lady knew a lot about that cat. She said the cat was washed overboard in a storm, but it managed to find a rope and clamber up it. This is strong evidence that cats have nine lives.

I had forgotten that Bass was eventually lost at sea in 1803, somewhere in the Pacific Ocean up to the north of Australia. Neither he nor his boat has ever been found. Flinders was captured by the French at Mauritius and kept there for seven years because the English and the French were at war. Both men were married, but spent many years apart from their wives, who were back in England.

There were maps on show, some of them showing parts of the Tasmanian coast still unmapped.

There were also some small boats that were from the Boy Scouts – Sea Scouts. They dated from the 1960s and seventies. I had been in the Boy Scouts in the 1960s, and I remembered meeting Sea Scouts at big scouting events, but theirs was another world.

I enjoyed exploring the boats and the associated histories in the museum. I am not attracted to sailing, but the *Norfolk* was a beautifully made replica. It is made of Huon Pine, and the top few planks of the sides are made of Celery Top Pine. These trees were pointed out to us when I was on the Tarkine walk.

You could climb down the ladders into the hold of the *Norfolk*; there were three sections. There were bunks, and as little space above and below each bunk as possible. I can't imagine what that would be like, especially when the ship was rolling and waves were crashing over the boat.

My enthusiastic informant, the older lady at reception, told me there was one episode when the boat (this one, the replica, not Bass and Flinders' original) was hit by a wave taller than the mast, so the wave was over forty feet high. The boat rolled on its side, and two men were lost. However, the boat has five tons of lead in the hull, and it bobbed back upright, and so the boat and the rest of the crew got back to shore.

As I said, I am not attracted to sailing. However, I can appreciate bravery in exploits.

Square 24

"Here you are," said Lilian, "being a simple tourist, seeing interesting things, and you managed to tie it to your family's history, even if it was remote family." She laughed.

"But I did see interesting things," I protested. "I've always thought that the exploits of Bass and Flinders were extraordinary. They completely circumnavigated Tasmania and Australia in small boats at the beginning of the nineteenth century. The seas around Australia are not a pond. They can be wild. The story about the replica boat *Norfolk* reinforced that truth."

"But you found connections," she replied. "Even the Sea Scouts evoked some resonance in you."

"Yes, true, but there is a strong association there, even if it is one step removed."

"Yes, you said you were never in the Sea Scouts."

"I was in the Boy Scouts, and that is still a strong association."

"Why?"

"Because it was in the Scouts while I was a boy that I encountered respect for the bush, for trees and wildlife, and for the wilderness. That still runs deep for me, and in this modern life, it runs counter to how our society acts. The Scouts' creed tells me I am not alone, and I am not crazy."

"I thought the scouting movement was imperialist, militarist, royalist and masculinist, in other words, the epitome of all the values that were in the ascendancy when it was founded, in the early 1900s. I am surprised at you."

"I suppose all of those things are true, but they weren't the things that were central for me. The thing that resonated for me was the respect for bush. If you want to argue about the Scouts, I can only say that what I got from it was a creed that said, 'When you go into the bush, respect everything. Take only what you need to keep yourself alive, and take nothing with you out of the bush.' Later, when cameras became part of life, the creed was amended to say, 'You can take photos!' This only underlined the creed more strongly."

"If I wanted to argue with you," said Lilian, "I could say that that was a romantic notion suitable for boys. It wasn't meant for grown-ups."

I smiled. "And I would have to argue with you. I remember when I was only about ten, and I was still in the Cubs, that one night the lady who was the Cub leader, the Akela, whose real-life name was Florence Wilkes, read a message to us. It was Baden-Powell's last message to the Boy Scouts, at a World Jamboree when he was eighty. She read it as if Baden-Powell was sitting right there and addressing each of us in person. And the last words of the message were: 'Stick to your Scout Promise always – even after you have ceased to be a boy.'"

"You remember that?"

"I do. She read it so solemnly, as if it were a message that was solid enough for all time, and for all of our lives."

"And what is the promise?"

"On my honour, I promise that I will do my duty to God and the Queen, to help other people, and to keep the scout law."

"And you still believe this?"

"The elements have evolved, but there is an essence that I have not rejected and will never reject. I think it awoke me to the seriousness and wonder of being alive. I was a person who had honour to keep, who could make a promise and keep it, and who could aim to do good in the world, or fail to. I grew up that night."

"You said the elements have evolved?"

"Baden-Powell grew up as an Englishman in the age of the Empire, and as a Christian, so of course the beliefs and ideas of the Boy Scouts reflect that. But even he had to change, because boys soon came along from other countries and religions to join the Scouts, so either he was going to have to exclude them or make room for them. Even girls came along, and he hadn't anticipated that.

"When the very first Scout Rally was held at the Crystal Palace in 1909, a number of girls appeared in Scout uniform, and told

Baden-Powell that they were the 'Girl Scouts'. The Girl Guides movement was soon started, with Baden-Powell's sister.

"It is now understood in the Scouts that the Christian God is better generalised to 'spiritual beliefs'. This is a big step, because the traditional Christian position is that all other religions are wrong. Remember the preacher I told you about at Port Arthur who spent two hours each Sunday roaring at the congregation about how the Irish Roman Catholics were going to burn in the fires of Hell?"

"Yes," said Lilian. "I agree; that is a massive shift. God has to become bigger, and be understood as the essence of meaning and love in the world, not as a specified being that belongs to a given group of people."

"Well, that's a quick lesson in theology!" I had to say. "I still think the current words are a compromise, because once you express it how you just did, it becomes more a question of understanding and the heart, not a set of cognitive beliefs that lend themselves to argument."

"What about your duty to the Queen?"

"Well, amusingly, it's the same Queen! It's been the same Queen since I was two years old."

"Yes, but...? You said the Scouts movement has members from all around the world. And besides, the Empire is over."

"Indeed it is, so instead of my duty to the Queen (who is now, by the way, the Queen of Australia), a Boy Scout promises to contribute to their community and to the world. I like this change. Much as I am sceptical that anything is bigger and better these days, I think this statement is bigger and better. And I imagine Scouts from different countries standing shoulder to shoulder reaffirming that promise."

"And the promise that said 'Help other people'. Has that been changed?"

"No. It is the same. I think the point is that Baden-Powell was aware that many people grow up and consume themselves in striving for their own success and for money. He said the simple thing – money won't make you happy, but helping other people will help make you happy. That truth hasn't changed, and it was in that last statement that Akela read to us young Cubs."

"What about the Scout's Law? What is that?"

"A lot of abstract nouns!" I laughed.

"But the law must say something! What does it say?"

"It says what you'd expect it to say – be respectful, be considerate, care for others, care for the environment, do what is right, and so on. It's like when Aborigines talk about the law; you know they know what the law is; they don't have to spell it out. It's part of us, when we are not being greedy or cruel or dishonest or egotistical.

"I think that, when I was in the Scouts, I didn't try to memorise it. I read the book that Baden-Powell wrote in 1908 for the Scouting movement – "Scouting for Boys". That was to imbibe the law. And I practised it by learning skills in Scouting activities. An essential aspect of the Law was to learn and develop, and to face challenges with courage."

"Did all that come back from looking at boats in a museum?"

I nodded, then remembered that Lilian was on the phone. "Yes, it did. And I wonder how fortunate I was to have experienced everything I did in the Scouts. Just to belong to a group that said there is such a thing as honour, and to stand up straight and own it. Do you think many people have missed out on that?"

Lilian thought about this, then she said, "That's probably true, which is unfortunate, but there are also people who took on the beliefs in that simple, childlike way but who have not been able to refine them the way you have. For example, for them, duty to the Queen still has to be taken literally. They would think you have betrayed your promise. Sadly."

"Yes, I see. And yes, that is sad. For all that, I don't want that to diminish the reality and the value of what I and many others boys got from the Scouts. It gave each of us a foundation for living adult life as a decent person."

"Oh," said Lilian, "I think this is a square."

Square 25

"Where are you on your trip?" asked Lilian.

"I stayed at a bed-and-breakfast place just north of Hobart. It was a place called New Town. Tasmanians have not yet contracted place names into one word. If it were Sydney, we would call it Newtown. That aside, the house was lovely. It was a two-storey house in a 'good' part of town. All the houses were statements to the community of the time."

"What is it?" asked Lilian. "Did something stand out?"

"Yes, exactly. I had trouble finding the place. There was no sign on the street, and not even the number was evident on the street. I even cold-called a house to try and get some information. I met a middle-aged woman and her teenage son, and although they were nice, they had no information to offer. Eventually I found a driveway between some bushes that went up to a car park, and this was the place.

"Not too tragic, then?" said Lilian.

"In terms of travel and what it might throw up, no," I smiled.

"So, what was interesting?"

"For a start, I loved the house. It was an elegant edifice, two stories high, in this elegant neighbourhood. I knock on the door, and a man in his fifties answers. He says his name is Saed (he spells it) and he has owned this place for fifteen years. He is enthusiastic. He is pleased to see me. I think he might be Lebanese or Egyptian. He asks me if I know Mary Reibey."

"I don't know," says Lilian. "Who is Mary Reibey?"

"It was the most unexpected question. But I know who she is," I said, "because she is significant. I told you about William Archer, my William Archer. And I told you the story about how he said he maintained he was a free settler, not a convict. My mother's story, the story she told me, that she believed, although I now know otherwise."

"Yes," she said. "So?"

"I believe the source of that story in colonial days was Mary Reibey. She had been a convict in the very early days in Sydney. But after her sentence ended, she went back to England for a visit to her family, and then she come back out to Sydney. Soon after that there was a Census, and one of the questions was about your status – convict, ex-convict or free settler. She answered that she was a free settler – she had come to Sydney as a free settler.

"And technically, it was true. And I think this was the precedent for William Archer to maintain that he was a free settler, after he had been back to England in the 1860s then come back to Australia. So, for family reasons, Mary Reibey is big – she is a myth maker!"

"There's more to Mary Reibey, isn't there?"

"Indeed, there is. She was a very good business woman. Apart from many other significant business dealings, she was one of the initial stockholders of the Bank of New South Wales, now Westpac. Her importance is acknowledged by the fact that her face is on the twenty-dollar note."

"Okay. That is recognition that is unquestionable. Are you going to tell me there is a connection with the house you stayed in?"

"Yes, that's what I am going to tell you. Saed told me the house was built in 1897 by a grandson of Mary Reibey. Clearly he was excited that a random guest knew about her."

"Don't tell me – you were excited too?"

"Obviously. But it was also exciting that the owner of the house actually knew its history and thought that was something to get excited about."

"Fair enough."

"Are you going to ask me what I had for dinner?"

"No, but I am happy for you to tell me."

"I was in the middle of a suburb. How was I going to find somewhere to eat?"

"I think you are an intelligent man, but did you figure it out?"

"Yes. There were some restaurants about half a kilometre away, according to Google Maps, so I walked there. I found a Malay restaurant. I was happy about that. I went in and ordered a meal, and then the lady said I could have a glass of wine. I was unsure about the import of this statement."

"So am I," said Lilian, and I knew she was smiling.

"The lady pointed up to a blackboard, which had writing on it in chalk. Aside from the meal options, there was a list of wines of different varieties. The lady then told me that it was Friday, and I could order a glass of wine. I had no idea what this meant. Apart from anything else, there was a language barrier, and I didn't want to push that too far. I could not deny that it was Friday, and I thought that this was clearly an event that was worth celebrating. I decided that I would drink a glass of sauvignon blanc, and told her so. She was very pleased."

"So, it is still a mysterious world," said Lilian.

"There is no doubt about that, but the food was good. So was the wine."

"How should we classify this story?" Lilian asked. "There is the quilt to think of, you know."

I laughed. "You know I am leaving the quilt up to you."

"Are you?" she said, and I realised that I had not said this explicitly before. I was silent, not being sure of the significance of what I had said.

I also realised that there were angry, scared parts of me, that did not want to hand over this kind of control to another person.

"What?" she said.

"Nothing," I said.

"I see," she replied.

"Oh," I sighed.

"What?" she said, again.

"Can we just leave it?" I asked.

"Yes, but not forever. Well, we can, but that would be a failure."

"It's not Friday," I replied.

"True, but one day it will be," she retorted. "Once in every seven days, it is Friday."

"I've got another story to add to this one. It's also about dinner and restaurants."

"Yes, I want to know now. I want to know where it fits in," said Lilian.

"Of course it fits in," I said abruptly, "but that wasn't the point at the time."

"Okay," she soothed, "but tell me."

"I was staying at the same place, Mary Reibey's grandson's house. It was another night, and I found a Thai place to eat, a bit more than half a kilometre away. The weather was uncertain, so I put on my good jacket that I'd bought in Ireland, and set off. It poured raining most of the way there. The jacket was good, but my trousers were soaked. There weren't many people in the restaurant. Closest to me was a group of three people, a couple visiting from the north coast of New South Wales, and a local lady. They were all in the university sector. I say 'sector' with some distaste.

"Their conversation was audible, and they talked about projects and relationships and the current culture of universities. I understood it; I wasn't warmed by any of it. The meal was good. There was no wine, because it was a bring-your-own kind of place. When I stood to leave, the man said he hoped I had not been disturbed by their conversation. What could I say? I responded to him politely.

"I walked home in the sunset, with the rain ended. The light was liquified and golden. I walked past a sports ground, one that was geared for crowds, with a grandstand. There had been no game on today.

"It was later that I learned, from going back to my notes about Sarah Crosby, that the sports ground used to be Brickfields Hiring Depot, and that Sarah had spent time here, waiting to be picked for an appointment as servant to a free settler's house. It aches, every time. However, on the way back to Mary Reibey's grandson's place, I stopped at the perfect time to take a sunset photo of Mount Wellington."

Lilian was silent. I was getting used to the idea of her planning a quilt out of my squares.

Square 26

When I went to Tasmania in 1973, I was just pleased to be able to walk without the assistance of crutches or a walking stick. Despite the fact that I had been in the Boy Scouts and I had been on many serious bushwalks, in December 1973 I would not have been up to the same sort of caper. I had had the motor bike accident in January, and had spent most of the year with bones being mended, and skin grafts taking place. I had been getting patched up. Parts of my body look like a patchwork quilt.

When I left work early this year, I did the kinds of things you should do when you leave work: fix things at home that you have been neglecting for a long time. Accordingly, I determined to paint a section of fence that should have been white but looked quite shabby. I prepared methodically, and located an old pile of newspapers in the garage so I could put down sheets of newspaper and not have drops of paint on the concrete.

My eye fell on an article in one of the newspapers. This is always the danger of undertaking tasks at home; you discover distractions and find yourself making a cup of tea instead so that you can sit down and read. The newspaper was seven years old. The article was about bushwalking in Tasmania in the Tarkine wilderness on the west coast. I made a cup of tea.

I did finish painting the fence, and it looks very white. However, before I got back to that, I did an internet search on walking in the Tarkine. Happily, the trekking company that was talked about in the article was still going strong, and was taking bookings for the spring. Before I got back to painting the fence, I had booked my place on a trek. I got a lot of satisfaction painting that fence – it was like making a blank canvas. I didn't know what else I would do in Tasmania, but this was a start. I would build my trip around the trek.

* * * * *

We met in the lobby of a grand hotel in Launceston at 7:30 AM. There was humour in the juxtaposition of a group of people preparing to go bush with groups of people who were dressed up for a day's intense tourism, or suited up for a day of business affairs. We loaded our bags into the trailer and hopped into the twelve-seater bus. There were ten of us plus one of the guides. The other guide was going to meet us when we got there.

We left around eight o'clock and drove west for about two hours. I had little idea where we were going other than place names and 'west'. The weather looked sort of fine, but it was changing a lot, with clouds and wind. The first rule of this trip, obviously, was not to count on fine weather, or even to care about that.

We got to a tiny town called Waratah and met the other guide. We had a bush morning tea in the park, with the water boiled for tea and coffee on a small gas burner. Looking at us from a short distance away was a waterfall. It had a strong flow, and fell into a valley maybe fifty feet or more. Someone said that this is the only town that has a waterfall in town. It is certainly the only waterfall I have ever seen in a town, over the road from the general store.

The café/store was a cosy wooden place with a fire going in the mid-morning in late spring, and a few bush handicrafts for sale. One old guy with a massive grey beard came out of the café for a chat with us. He said he had worked in the nearby tin mine when it was going. He had bought pieces of land when they came up for sale, and he now had about five acres. The cheapest one cost him $500. I thought, if I had worked in a tin mine and let my beard grow long, I could be him. What's the difference? Sometimes it doesn't seem like much.

After morning tea, we drove a short distance to see what the old guy had been talking about. We stopped and walked up a short track. On the way we saw rusty machinery lying around, like dogs in their master's den, warming their bellies by the fire and waiting for the next exploit to start. At the end of the trail we were looking straight at the side of a mountain that had been carved away in shelves, and the bare earth was a splatter of different reds and browns – tin ore. This was Mount Bischoff.

We learned history. The tin had been discovered by an eccentric man, the bushman and prospector called James 'Philosopher' Smith in 1871. This had led to the establishment of a tin mine, and the rough town called Corinna on the banks of the Pieman River. It was the place where the wild funeral was held in 1897 for the publican Gam Webster.

The mine generated lots of money for the Tasmanian colony and at the time it saved the state from having to hand over its sovereignty to Victoria. The tin was sold to English manufacturers. The mine ran until just after World War II. As with many mines, the idea is always there that it could reopen if the price of tin increases enough to make it likely that the mine would turn a profit.

This is history, the facts. Tin was in demand, and this location was a productive source of tin. It was necessary for half a mountain to be carved away for the purpose. It didn't matter that there were landslides, or that the watercourse was filled with mud and metals. That was collateral damage. In the great scheme of things, this is one small area. And it will recover, or that's the mythology.

To make an omelette, you have to be prepared to break eggs. We use tin, and it has to come from somewhere, and also, it can't come from just anywhere, it has to come from the places where tin is found. We are familiar with the arguments. Our lives are located within these arguments, entirely surrounded. We assume the presence of tin in our lives, and even if this were not so, if we had found a substitute, nothing has changed. We are beneficiaries of mining.

In my family, on my father's side, mining was always a facet of life. They came from Cornwall, and tin mining for them probably went back at least three thousand years. I have to accept it, don't I? Mining is something societies have always done. But, there is no longer any tin mining in Cornwall. Why is this?

My answer is, in the nineteenth century, the power of machines was put to work in mines, and in less than fifty years, the mines were exhausted. Again, price was an accompanying factor, because cheaper tin was being brought into England from mines elsewhere in the world, including Tasmania. However, the fact seems to be that the harnessing of fossil energy to run machines led to the mines being exhausted. The thing that was seen as a great blessing – machines that replaced human effort – was a curse. And I think this is the conundrum of our society that we have not faced.

There is also the conundrum that in order to maintain the accoutrements of our society – buildings, comforts and transport – we have to use up the natural resources of the world and make mountains ugly. We step around this question as if it were a mere curiosity, just as we stood there in the bush and gazed at the colours of the tin ore in its unprofitable stage.

* * * * *

When I was in Hobart, I went to MONA, the Museum of Old and New Art. It is about 10 kilometres up the Derwent River. It is quite an adventure for the senses. It is an extraordinary vision and must have cost a huge amount to build. It has been carved directly out of the ground and it goes down five levels. When you are down at the bottom, you can see the saw marks in the walls of the giant circular saws that were used to cut the stone out to make the space.

One of the temporary exhibits (temporary meaning about six months) is called 'Mine', which is about mining, by a New Zealand-born, Berlin-based artist, Simon Denny. The exhibit includes large mock-ups of traditional mining equipment – excavators and such like – made of what looked like cardboard. The entire room was a game board, as if you were in the middle of a game being played.

There were stacks of boxes that were like a boxed children's game, and the game is called 'Extractor'. It is overwhelmingly mechanist in spirit; humans have been abstracted out of the picture. I take it that this is Denny's perspective on modern society; our society is fundamentally based on extraction. Simply calling the exhibition 'Mine' points out the great irony of that word. A mine takes what is in the earth, what is not yours, and calls it 'mine'. 'Mining' is the process of making it 'mine'.

Denny sees us taking this approach into the future. There are references to mining other planets for their minerals. He also makes a metaphorical leap, to talk about the new frontier of 'big data' and 'data mining'. Clearly, he is saying that we are going forward into this future with the same attitude that leaves ruined natural landscapes in its wake.

The only way to experience such an exhibition is through disassociation. It is like the mother saying to her child who is looking at a cat-o-nine-tails whip, "Oh, look, this one doesn't have any barbs on the ends of the cords", as if it were a curiosity, and not refer to the fact that the whip is for shredding the skin off a man's back. The giant room was saying, "We are the Extractors! We will take everything because we can."

I think of the Aboriginal way of life in contrast. Their relationship to life was to ensure that anything they took or used was replaceable, and would be replaced. If not, it was in endless supply, for as many generations to come as there had been ancestors. Food for the body, wood for the fire, bark for the canoe, all would be replenished. Stone to shape for the tips of spears, nothing compared to what was there.

Many would argue that extraction and mechanisation have given us modern civilisation. Any unsavoury aspect of this civilisation is explained as 'the price of progress'. These are the loose, shabby arguments of those who have power, of those who have conquered and don't need to be careful about being correct. In Denny's vision of an invincibility that is inhuman, victory is assured, but there is no life in the city of victory, just endless boxes of a game called Extractor, so that the children can learn the essential philosophy at a young age.

Life is made of gentler stuff. It survives through collaboration with life. I asked one of the attendants if she found the exhibition disturbing or depressing. She said she supposed so.

Outside the subterranean building there were other dark moments. There was a collection of old boilers, which may have had some industrial purpose in the early twentieth century. They looked abandoned, and they were covered with graffiti, the kind that suggests anger and violence. One statement said: "Look back on pathos and failure." Clearly, those who survive must be tough and mean.

There was another building that had a glass wall, and you could look inside. Stacked in the middle of the floor were vertical piles of what could have been sheets of slate. They could also have been sheets of petrified paper, or glass. They were all grey, the distressing grey of ruin and abandonment. The floor around this was covered by smashed shards of the same material, all blanketed with the same appalling grey dust. A couple of metres away, behind a cordon, there were several people looking at it all and wondering. They were obviously visitors like me, but although I walked all around the vicinity, I could not see how you could get into that space. It seemed appropriate.

After this experience, viewing these disturbing visual inventions and many more, the obvious thing to do was to have a meal and a drink, but I could not, not in this place. I got back onto the ferry and left, and I did not eat until I got back to Hobart.

Square 27

I was keen to talk to Lilian after I sent her this square. I had had the idea that I would be talking about the trek in the Tarkine wilderness, which sounded refreshing, but when I started, the episode with the tin mountain had intervened. That had led me to the 'Mine' exhibition at MONA. It was dark.

"I'm sorry," I said to her. "So far it hasn't worked out well. It's as if I have fallen into a pit."

"Ah," she said. "Your artistic expedition seems to have presented you with dark visions, which have been mirrored by your outdoor pursuits."

"I know we are supposed to believe in progress, and the rightness of it, apart from its inevitability. But the world seems increasingly doomed to be catastrophic. I want to whisper in somebody's ear, 'I never believed.'"

"I'll keep your secret," Lilian laughed. Then she said, "I'm laughing because I can relate to the image of perfectly stacked sheets of glass that are collapsing and smashed, and covered with appallingly grey dust."

That simply confirmed the darkness, its reality and its oppressiveness. I didn't respond.

"But you did go on the walk?" she asked. "Was it good?"

"Yes, it was," I confessed readily. When I didn't try and reconcile the two, and just focused on the walk, it was good. It was refreshing. Then I remembered to speak. "It stood on its own. I had to focus, because it was strenuous, and at times I was heaving for air walking up hundreds of steep steps to the tops of mountains. It didn't allow me to indulge in speculative thoughts about the future of the world."

"Okay," Lilian smiled (I knew she was smiling). "So just tell me about that."

* * * * *

I will start again. I went on a three-day walk in the Tarkine wilderness in the west of Tasmania, in a group of a dozen people, which included two guides. We drove two hours west of Launceston. I learned that the Tarkine wilderness is not a national park, it is a reserve. The word 'reserve' doesn't mean it is protected from 'development', it means the area is reserved by the government for its purposes, so it can be logged or mined at any time if the government thinks it is expedient (meaning, profitable) to do that. That little fact sharpened our experience of what we encountered over the three days.

I was feeling the strength of gratitude, along with trepidation. I would not have been able to do this in 1973 as my right leg was just recovering. A while ago, I found a photograph of myself on crutches, from my mother's collection. I didn't realise that this photo existed. The photo was taken just a couple of months before I went to Tasmania; my right leg is notably withered, from ten months of no use. So, gratitude for being able to do this walk now.

But I also felt trepidation, about whether or not I would be able to do this. I have worked in sedentary occupations for the last twenty years. Although I did yoga regularly, I did not do what they call, these days, aerobic exercise. Would I be physically capable of walking fifteen kilometres a day? I guessed that I would, but then there was the altitude to consider – could I be able to climb the heights that might be required? Or would I be one of those embarrassing 'elderly' people who have to be carried out on a stretcher?

My first feeling of comfort came from looking around the group. Most of them seemed to be in their sixties, and I thought I would be able to keep up with them. Secondly, the guides looked as if they were sensible. I have met crazy walkers who are driven to try to walk ten kilometres an hour for eight hours solid. I know what they look like. These guys looked human.

I did okay. I did get puffed on the steep climbs, and there were a quite a few of those, but I realised that I recovered quite quickly, and could go on, and it was a great relief to realise that, to know I could trust myself to get through a whole day and I would not feel ruined at the end of it. Back to basics. I was not thinking about the end of the world. I could be satisfied with today.

The first stint we did was a walk down to the Philosopher's Falls. Yes, they were named after James Philosopher Smith, who had discovered them. (I understand when I am saying this that they had been known for tens of thousands of years by the Aboriginal people of this place.)

We walked about 500 metres to the river bank then walked maybe a kilometre down to the falls. It was a good solid track with steel grid bridges and timber steps where this was needed. There were a hundred or so steps down to a platform on the side of the valley where you could look at the falls, which fell a good hundred feet below where we were. There was an old sluice beside the track – when the tin mine was going, this gave them controlled water for running machinery and washing dirt and ore.

We were in rainforest, moist and green, canopy overhead, and the water in the river gushed enthusiastically. It felt good. The people in the group were polite, and interested in things, but not too talkative. It was pleasant. One felt that a rhythm would develop. The guides had periodic sessions where they pointed things out or explained the history of the place, but they did not talk incessantly. You could also see they were learning to work with each other, and that was good to watch too.

We only carried light packs, no food or utensils or overnight gear. This was a sensible way to explore.

In the afternoon, we got to the place where we would stay for the next two nights, Corinna. The name Corinna is the Aboriginal word for the river. It is also their word for the thylacine, the extinct Tasmanian Tiger.

Yes, Gam Webster's wild funeral had been held here in 1897. The old pub is still there (closed up), and a couple of other old buildings, just small houses really. There is a new building which is the general store plus bar plus restaurant, with a verandah right along the front.

In front of the general store is a car park for boating people, and a punt that can take you the fifty metres across the Pieman River. This place is a one-hour boat trip from the ocean. All the roads are gravel. There are some cabins, which are where we stayed. There is electricity, and a satellite dish. All around there is forest. In the evening there was the sound of a generator, but it stopped around ten o'clock, and then it was silent all night.

People come here to fish and play with boats, or just to camp. We are in the hills.

We deposited our gear in the cabins then went for a walk for about an hour, down along the river than back around in a big circle. The forest was beautiful, but quite different from the rainforests of northern New South Wales that I am familiar with, in the Border Ranges National Park. The main trees in the Tarkine are myrtles, not eucalypts. I learned that these myrtles are called *Nothofagus cunninghamii*; they are not related to English myrtles at all. But they reminded me of the Antarctic Beeches in the Border Ranges, which I knew are called *Nothofagus moorei*.

All of these trees seemed ages old. They seemed older than the Ents in *Lord of the Rings*. They had acquired layers of strength, and secrets. One felt sure they could communicate.

While on our walk, we saw a pademelon quite close; it was not perturbed by us, and looked at us impassively. I got a photo. It was late afternoon and the light was lovely, complex and soft.

We had dinner in the restaurant, the twelve of us seated at one big table. We drank wine and talked about many things. Older people, if they are not rigid with opinions, are gentler than youth, calmer. I was reminded of my time in 1973 in youth hostels, when opinions and presumed knowledge were a much higher-stakes game.

My cabin was comfortable, roomy, with a little kitchen, a decent bathroom, and a warm Queen-size bed. I slept the sleep of those who have walked solidly in the day.

Square 28

"I am going to call this a square," I told Lilian.

"But there is more?" she asked.

"Yes, but you remember that saying: 'The day is sufficient unto itself'?"

"I do. So be it."

"Yes, that day was sufficient unto itself. I had started the morning in a Four-Star hotel in a city, and by evening I had walked into a rainforest and seen a waterfall, climbed up and down lots of steps, and I was staying next to a river in the middle of a forest. And I had been reconnected with trees that seemed infinitely old."

"Reconnected! Mmm. That was enough for a day, I think. But I do want to hear about the next day."

* * * * *

The crew prepared some breakfast for us in a picnic shed – cut-up fruit, yoghurt, muesli. Good enough. The weather was dark and threatening. We drove a short distance from Corinna and left the bus near a bridge over a river called the Savage River. We walked through forest. Again I was struck by the difference between this forest and the Border Ranges. This forest was open underneath the canopy, and the light was lighter. The rain came and went. We began walking upwards and parts of it were steep. In some sections there were steps, but mostly it was zigzag.

Once it got higher, we came out of the forest onto open scrub that was only a metre or so high; there were no trees anymore. It was cold and windy now, and I was pleased for my warm jacket, the one I had bought in Ireland, and the first serious pair of walking shoes I had bought in forty years. We were walking to the top of Mount Donaldson. It took about two hours.

I took photos. I realised that taking a photo gave you a chance to stop and get your breath back. I became more studious about my photos. At every step we were reminded that it was still spring, because the extent and variety of the flowers on the bushes was wonderful, far more marvellous than my meagre imagination could invent.

The last climb was taken with tired steps, but suddenly, there we were with a full-circle view, and the rusty fallen remains of a trig station at our feet. But, as one of the men said, they are not really needed anymore, given the new technologies. At that point my phone pinged – remember, I am walking with my phone because it is my camera, and as a bonus it has a compass. My phone pinged, meaning that at this high point in the middle of the wilderness I had reception, and I received a message.

The message was not from friends or family – they knew I was not contactable; it was from a real estate agent back in the Sydney suburb where I live, telling me that there was a house auction on today, and it was not too late to put in a bid for the property.

Apart from the wonders of mobile phone reception, the summit presented a gorgeous view. At one point I could see right to the coast; I could see the sea. Looking down, I could see the thread of the river, and two boats were making their way along, sweeping fans of water behind them. It was forest all the way to the horizon in every direction, with the exception of one scarred area which one of the guides said was a mining site.

As I looked longer, the nuances of the view clarified. I looked around in all directions; there was a constant shifting of the light. I saw this again later, when I looked at my photos. There were photos I had taken less than a minute apart, and the light in them was completely different. You would have thought it was a different day or a different place. Overall it was cold and dark, although it was only mid-morning, and the clouds looked ominous, manoeuvring for position and threatening to pour down. But there was a calm among the group, recognising that we were in an uncommon moment, briefly exalted and awed.

I think we ate mandarins up there. It was some kind of offering, while we watched the pockets of mist clinging to the heads of valleys and the dark change to light and back.

Walking down the same way, the clouds and mist continued to play and mingle, and occasionally it rained. It has been said that when you climb to the top, remember what you see up there, because you won't be able to see it anymore when you are back down below. But remembering will help you to understand where you are, back down below. It gives you a perspective from the point of view of the whole.

We walked all the way down again, back through the forest and back to the bus. We had lunch next to the river and drank hot tea. Then it seemed to be a simple matter of walking back to Corinna, following the Savage River. However, it was not so simple. You can't just follow the edge of the river; you end up climbing up into a multitude of gullies and down again, and there is mud and steepness to contend with. In some parts, we climbed right to the ridge-top. Occasionally there was a rope to haul yourself up with as you climbed.

The Danish explorer, Jorgen Jorgenson, had been here once. I knew about him only by having found, by accident, a book called *The English Dane*, and I was thereby acquainted with his remarkable, even improbable, life. This was a man who, for a period of a few weeks, was the King of Iceland. He was a seaman, naval captain, writer, merchant and speculator, and a friend of Sir Joseph Banks. His adventures included a voyage from Denmark in 1827 to explore the still largely unknown island of Van Diemen's Land. And thus he came ashore and explored the spot where we were.

On a sign board at Savage River, near where we ate lunch, this passage from Jorgenson was recorded: "Fallen trees in every direction had interrupted our march, and it is a question whether any human beings, either civilised or savage, had ever visited this savage-looking country. Be that as it may, all about appeared well-calculated to arrest the progress of any traveller, sternly forbidding man to traverse those places which nature had selected for its own silent and awful repose."

The board went on to say that Jorgenson's party covered just three kilometres in one day, and were forced to spend the night in scrub by the Donaldson River in a south-westerly gale and heavy showers. Our path, in contrast, had been fashioned for us. The ropes were placed to help walkers at awkward spots. Hundreds of wooden steps had been built to get you up and down the really steep parts.

And yet it was hard; it was strenuous. At one point we came to a pontoon anchored to the bank, and we stopped there to have some fruit. Again the light was changing rapidly. I took a photo of a tree opposite the pontoon that shone like silver against the dark green of the trees behind it. It was vivid, like the burning bush that Moses saw. But the next minute the light was gone; the tree looked just like the other trees. If I didn't have the photo, I might not believe it.

We saw many, many small miracles along the way – mosses, fungi, flowers, strange growths that I didn't have names for, way up on the trunks of trees. There was one tree, a myrtle, where we all stopped to take photos. It was more a sculpture than a tree, and we all climbed in among the convolutions of its trunk to have more photos taken, as if the tree was allowing us to celebrate with it. We were all wet and muddy; you could see the delight in our faces.

When we got back to Corinna, we showered and changed, and got to the restaurant for dinner clean and fresh. We turned the heaters on in our cabins and dried our clothes for tomorrow.

Square 29

"Lilian," I said, "I'm going to need another square. This one is just Day 2. There's still Day 3, and that was different. I can't just say 'Ditto'."

"I won't argue with you about squares," she replied. "Carry on. Accumulate."

"It won't go on forever. It will come to an end."

"Sure, like a quilt."

* * * * *

Day 3. We got up early. We had to get onto the boat by 6:30 am, so breakfast came after we had got on board. At first it looked as if the boat was not going to start, and I could see that the guide was already thinking of alternatives. He was a quick thinker. The diesel motor kept ticking over sluggishly, as if it had no intention of being kicked out of bed; but at last it belched reluctantly into life. The captain seemed resigned either way.

This was our one-hour trip down to the mouth of the river. We were accompanied by a six-person group from another trekking company; our schedules needed to work with the ferryman's. The Pieman River was about 50 metres wide, and placid. It is tidal up to where we were, at Corinna.

The valley is steeply V-shaped, and the ferryman said the river was up to 120 metres deep, which I have trouble believing. I can't make sense of it. My guess was about six to ten metres. The forest comes all the way down to the water, so it feels utterly timeless, like Joseph Conrad going deep into the heart of Africa. There is a middle-aged American couple in the other group, which adds to the feeling of being in a strange country, not at home anymore.

The captain stopped the boat to show us a tree fern that was special; it had a tall thin trunk and there are not many of them around. He let the boat drift around in a circle so that everyone could see. Without the putt-putt of the motor, it was awfully quiet. Was this the 'silent and awful repose' that Jorgenson and his men had experienced?

Eventually, the question about the pieman had to be addressed: Why was this called the Pieman River? While the guide had some time on his hands, as the captain resumed his stoic oversight of the boat's gentle putt-putt voyage to the coast, he told us the story.

The relevant person was a baker in England, but he had a fight with someone and killed him, so he cooked his flesh and put it into pies. As a convict, he was known as the pieman. He was imprisoned at Macquarie Harbour, and he escaped. He was eventually captured in this river valley, and the river became known as Pieman River. It is a weird story in many respects, but that seems to be the way of the west coast.

The part about human flesh in pies, whether it was supposed to be in England or in the convict colony, has apparently been proven to be false. One suspects that he would have been hung if the story had been true. The identity of the convict seems to be certain. He was Thomas Kent of Southampton, a pastry-cook who was transported to Van Diemen's Land in 1816. And he was indeed a troublesome convict, hence his banishment to Macquarie Harbour.

In the end, the river is named after the nickname of a convict, and that's a story in itself.

This is the same country that Jorgenson later found to be all but impenetrable. Why did the guards pursue the pieman? I thought the main idea of Macquarie Harbour was that there was nowhere for convicts to go if they escaped. The past has all manner of good stories, but not very often an appropriate explanation.

Another fact I learned: if you go out of the mouth of the Pieman River and go due west, you do not hit Africa. You are far to the south of it. You keep going, and you do not hit shore until you cross the Atlantic Ocean and get to the east coast of South America – Argentina. We actually carry a very simplistic image of the world inside our heads.

We came to the mouth of the river, well, a few hundred metres inside the mouth, where we disembarked. There was no jetty. We put a stepladder down on the rocks, and the captain revved the motor sufficiently to keep the boat in one spot, and we climbed down one at a time.

Boats don't usually go in or out of the mouth of the river. It is too dangerous most of the year. Last year they managed to get this boat out to take it to Launceston for maintenance and repairs, but they don't intend to do it again. They will find an alternative.

We started walking towards the beach; we were going to walk along the beach and see how far we could get. Shortly, we came across a hostile-looking encampment with a big sign painted roughly that said the bush was for "MULTI-USE". I mentioned this much earlier. This was the place. The core activity of these sociable beings was quad bikes.

It was all rather belligerent. It was like saying you were going to use an area for nuclear weapon testing, but someone else could grow roses there if they wished. We didn't see the people, but later we came across places where they had been spinning around, doing donuts. Share that with your rose garden! Quad bikes are allowed on the southern shore of the river, but not the northern shore. But the tough guys had their own little pontoon which they used to ferry the quad-bikes across the river.

Later, when we came back to the boat, we saw four quad bikes on the southern shore. The people were all dressed the same, in white, led by a beach buggy, and we guessed it was a tour run by a tour company. It seemed incongruous: we had the bad boys on our side of the river, and there were the angels in white on the southern bank, all in a dutiful line, following the leader.

The vegetation along the beachfront was all low-lying, swept into smooth shapes by the wind. The bushes looked so neat; it was like a manicured garden. Everything was in flower, reminding us once again that it was spring. So many different colours, and flowers of different shapes and sizes. Beautiful. We stopped at a pebbly beach. The pebbles were so smooth and clean, they looked as if they had just come out of a washing machine. Walking on them, it felt as if they were metres deep. It was good to walk on.

At another spot, there were conglomerate rocks that looked like rocky road, big blobs of rock all stuck together. And the whole vicinity around them was made up of sheets of rock pushed up out of the ground at an angle – schist. There were sandy beaches with white sand. At one point, there were heaps of foam at the edge of the waves, which, we were told, occurs at certain times of the year when some animals are breeding (I don't remember the explanation). Big handfuls of it were blowing into the air.

We stopped at an overhanging rock right near the shore line and boiled some water for tea and coffee. We were fortunate for the overhang, as it was raining a little. Then we climbed up a short pile of rocks and looked down on the beach. One of the guides climbed up on top and stood up. It was a long way to fall. Some others climbed up and stood. I chose not to and felt fine about that.

We walked back to the place where the boat would pick us up. The guide showed us a midden area and talked to us about the Aborigines, the first peoples. This was where I learned that it was in this area that Aboriginal women were kidnapped by white men, and the Aboriginal women dived for abalone.

It was also in this area that the Aborigines had permanent shelters and even what could be called villages. This reinforced what I had seen at the museum in Launceston. During our walk we had passed several middens of broken shells. I thought middens were rubbish dumps and wondered why Aboriginal people cared about them. I had completely misunderstood what they meant. The shells tell us that these were places of cooking, eating and communing. The guide said that when the shells are white it means they have been in a fire, that is, cooked.

We got the boat back to Corinna. All our gear had been loaded into the trailer in the morning. We had a drink in the bar, then we set off in the bus to go back to Launceston. It was after dark when we arrived. Six of us were available for dinner. Given that it was late, and we had not had to slog through mud today, we didn't stop to have a shower; we just headed off to the restaurant in the clothes we were wearing. It seemed appropriate.

It was a good meal. We ate at a North Indian restaurant around the corner from the hotel. It was warm conversation. We were coming back from where we had been, and projecting towards where we were off to next, but we were happy to be together for a little while longer.

And so things end.

Square 30

Naturally I sent this square to Lilian. She rang me. "Is it over then?"

"Not quite," I told her. "It's like when you are juggling balls, and there could be one or two still up in the air."

"But it's starting to look like a quilt," she said. I sensed enthusiasm, and I was immediately on guard.

"It's a Tasmanian patchwork," she ventured.

"Arguably," I replied, defensively.

"So you're not ready yet?"

"There are still.... how shall I say? Squares."

"Well, you should produce them!"

"I wonder about this one. It is significant, I think, but why? It is from my 1973 diary. It was 31st December, New Year's Eve."

"I'm surprised you haven't told me this. You told me about the next day, the first of January 1974."

"Chronology doesn't always give you the truth."

"Okay."

* * * * *

31st December 1973 (from the diary)

It was New Year's Eve. I made my way downtown to Bellevue Hostel, looking for refugees from St Helens, and then out into the town. Because it was a special night, I found Paul straight away. He had been in intense pursuit of Olga, the chess player, who was working in a nearby restaurant. Olga travelled with Donna, and together they were a stand-alone theatre troupe, just for amusement. Paul was keen on connecting with Olga.

Paul and I, meantime, were listening to a pop-up pop concert in the street, complete with fuzzy amps and speakers that were practically inaudible. Then who should rush up but Ute? We all hugged joyously and we were off – dancing, grinning, shaking hands with strangers, shaking life by the tail.

Somewhere in the middle of all that I followed Paul down to find Olga and Donna at the restaurant. We drank beers and Paul tried to talk, but he was intent on waiting for Olga to show, and I left him there, having the sense that it was going to be a while yet.

I was flowing down the footpath and I was mimicking something out of a hippie free-love parade, but it was the night for it. The wayward spirits in the crowd were responsive, cheering and letting go their day-time sombre masks. I sang out: "Love and kindness" because tonight it might be heard.

Amazingly, threading my way through the crowd, I found Ute again. She was dancing with fervour, perspiring, spinning and kissing strangers, madcap and complete. Matina was near, and she had acquired a boyfriend. He was happy amongst all of us, dancing around. And there were two guys in "la-de-da" tuxedos and velvet bowties, raising the level of the ambience. And I also met Steve – Steve of Steve and Beckie and the panel-van, who had given me a lift twice down the east coast. We shook hands happily.

Twelve o'clock came. The New Year. The start of 1974, and, I realised, the end of the long year 1973. There was shouting, kissing, hugging, grinning and hand-shaking all around. An old guy with an RSL badge shook several hands multiple times, and someone called Tony shook my hand, along with John, who is the guide we met at Port Arthur, who tonight had a laugh like a used car salesman. It was incongruous. My face was sore from grinning and kissing. The guys were coming around to kiss Ute ("Oh, Glenn, isn't this beautiful?" in German accent, and yes, it's very beautiful!).

We were spinning again. My right leg should drop off, but it kept going, and the band started up again. This was a whirl that absorbed anything untoward. A drunk guy approached Ute and looked as if he was intent on devouring her, but she was lithe, and she slipped away easily. Another drunk guy came on to a local girl and was about to paw her crudely and edge her away from our crowd, but Ute came up to whisk him off while I told her that, no, he wasn't one of us, and it might be better if she found another partner, and then Ute was back.

For a while I lost Ute, but in a moment she was spinning up next to me, still grinning, and telling me about the kisses for the policemen ("It was such fun!"), even the one who looked like Josef Goebbels (funny coming from a German girl). But too soon, things were starting to wind down. People were starting to fade out and disappear from the square.

A group of us drove back to the hostel, singing along the way. For an evening we were invincible, and perhaps not eternal, but we were touched by the breath of eternity. I remember one very drunk guy just sitting there at the hostel, with his soft, curly hair, smiling, while others fed him coffee. Ute was still acrobatic, balanced on one man's knee while she was teasing another, like sunshine exuding out of gold.

It was like that when I left, around 1:30 AM, and made my way home quietly, although I was still soaring.

Square 31

"So, then, a good night," commented Lilian.

"It was a bit more than that," I said. "'And so things end'," I added, quoting myself.

"What was it that ended?" She asked, quite rightly.

"Perhaps it was Ute, the German girl, although, as you can see, she was a firecracker, and too much for me."

"That almost sounds like regret."

"We would have spun out before long. It would have been hapless. Kind of like Paul and Olga," I said.

"Yes, true. Firecrackers burn you, and remain cheerful."

"It was a fun night," I said, "one of the best."

"I am going to suggest to you how to understand that night," said Lilian, "and I think it's true. You had been twelve months trapped in a medical situation over which you had no control, where the only thing you could do was pray and hope for healing. And here you were, on the last day of the year, in a welcoming city, dancing in the streets, on two legs. It was fantastic."

I listened, and then I said, "Sufficient unto the day..."

We were still not ready to stitch the quilt.

* * * * *

During the Tarkine trek, one of the group, Mike, told a story about the 2009 fires in Victoria. The first thing he said was that it was extraordinary that the fires happened on the same day in February as the great fires of Tasmania in 1967 – 7th February. He wasn't the first person to have noted that fact.

Mike and his wife lived in the country on the southern coast of Victoria. They had built a house out of stone over a period of eight years. Mike was a left-brain thinker, sober, rational, methodical. They had written down a fire plan and when the fires came near, they followed the plan, item by item. They packaged up the precious items from the household that they would want to save if the worst came to the worst, and he sent his wife off with them, and he dressed for the eventuality, completely covered from head to toe with fire gear. Only his ears were exposed. After the event he realised that his ears had blistered.

He went through the steps of the plan. He watered the roof and filled up the gutters with water. Inside the house he had filled up the sinks and the bath with water, and shut all the windows. He had cleared any flammable debris from around the house. The fire was approaching. He had had word. And the fire came in a rush, and with a roar.

He raced inside and shut the door, but embers came in after him, and he had to put out several spot fires inside the house. He said the noise was incredible. The fire passed quite quickly, but the heat was incredible and when he went outside, everything in sight was black and smoking. Things that could melt had melted. The house was saved. His ears were blistered. The noise in his ears remained.

Afterwards, when the time of the fires was over, they moved back into the stone house, but neither of them ever felt safe, and little things that reminded him of the fire would set off his anxiety. They ended up selling the house (and 40 acres) and moving to the coast to live, and he said they are much happier. Mike was obviously affected deeply, even though he was telling this story calmly as we walked along, up hills and up steps to the top of a ridge.

Square 32

"That story obviously affected you," said Lilian.

"Yes, it did," I said. "It wasn't just the story, which was extreme enough. It was the fact that the person telling it was not an excitable man. He was calm and logical. If you were in a dangerous situation, you would want him by your side. He would keep you anchored and give you the best chance of surviving. But he had come face to face with a presence that was all-consuming. It does no good to reduce that to rationalistic terms. They don't measure up.

"And of course, the main message was that you can plan your life out sensibly and even nobly, and in a moment it can be gone, snuffed out completely. And then I think of all the people I have talked about – Sarah and Edward Lewis, the Tasmanian Archers, the cheerful youths of 1973 alongside their tortured desires, and the people I met on this trip. Not to be melodramatic, but it's a measure – what would it be worth if it were burnt to a crisp tomorrow?"

"Should I slash my wrists?" laughed Lilian, a little nervously.

"No, don't do that," I replied, disappointed that I had indeed been melodramatic. "I want to balance that story, which did indeed affect me deeply, with this image. On my flight back to Sydney – this time, we went over mountains. It had to have been northern Victoria. I looked down through the clouds and saw hard white, not clouds – it was snow on the mountains. I had never seen that before. It felt really special."

"So what are you saying? What did you get from that?"

"The things that amaze us are not the things we have made, not the results of our shiny plans, it is the stuff of nature, its vastness and its grandness."

"Okay. I get it."

"Can you sew that together?"

There, I had said it.

"Are there any more squares?" asked Lilian.

I laughed. "There is one, to complement the story I just told you about fire. It's about the 1967 fires in Tasmania."

* * * * *

While I was visiting the Cascades Female Factory in Hobart, I walked up the road to get some lunch. The place to go to was the Cascade Brewery; it had a café and bar across the road from the brewery. It also had a nice garden, a legacy of the glory days of the brewery, I imagine. (Yes, the brewery is Cascade without an 's'; the Female Factory is Cascades with an 's', and I don't know why.)

I discovered that the brewery ran tours, so I thought I should take the opportunity to do that. I got some lunch first, and then went on the tour.

The guide was a young Japanese lady. That was unexpected. I had to concentrate to understand her, but I got most of what she said. She was very well-informed. It seems that the Cascade Brewery is now owned by Asahi, the Japanese beer company, which had to explain the nationality of the guide. Later, when I got a chance to do my homework, I realised that this news was very fresh – agreement had only been reached for the sale in July 2019, and at the time of my tour, it had yet to be finalised. Asahi are buying the Australian entity, Carlton & United Brewery, of which Cascade is a part.

It was interesting to have the whole operation explained, and to see the factory in action, such as the conveyor belts along which the bottles raced on their way to be packaged, either in six-packs or cartons. We went up on the walkways above the huge vats (half a dozen of them, each of 100,000 litres) and looked right down to the bottom.

The guide told us the history of the place, going back to 1824 – the tour guide version. The founders were Peter Degraves and his brother-in-law, Major Hugh McIntosh. They started business as a sawmill, then in 1832 they moved into brewing. However, McIntosh died in 1834, and the company passed into the hands of Degraves. Both the milling and brewing operations expanded hugely after the gold rush commenced in Victoria in the 1850s. Later, many of the close relatives died when a ship taking them on a voyage back to England sank, but the company stayed in the Degraves family until it was bought up by a larger corporation in the twentieth century.

Now the 1967 fires come into the story. This was the catastrophic day in Tasmania when about one-third of the state's forests were burned out, 1,300 homes were destroyed and 62 people died. The fires near Hobart were terrible, and the Cascade factory was burnt out. It would have been understandable if the company's existence ended there. However, the owners were determined to rebuild the factory and get back to making beer as soon as possible.

Supported by the efforts of its employees and volunteers from the surrounding community, the facilities were rebuilt and became functional in just three months, and the first beer was ready by the beginning of May. The guide was quite passionate in telling this story, and I think it is a stirring story, the employees and the community refusing to be defeated by the devastation of the fires, and going all out to get the factory back into production in an unbelievably short period of time.

The fact that the product involved was beer no doubt helped – the ethos of beer, that it represents conviviality in a community. Then there was the longevity of the company – it went right back to the early days of the colony. As well, it had (and still has) a stunning building, a Gothic stone creation that looks like a giant wedding cake in the wilderness. And it has the magnificent backdrop of Mount Wellington. It all fires the imagination.

For all this, I couldn't help feeling a sense of incongruity, that this story was being told by a representative of a giant global corporation with an annual turnover in the hundreds of billions of dollars. At that level, companies are bought and sold regularly according to the prognostications of accountants. If the fire had happened today, it would have been solely an economic decision whether to reopen or stay closed for good. Sentiments about beer or local communities would not hold much sway.

After the tour, I drank three samples of their offerings: a cider, a lager and a stout. I drank them slowly as I talked with a young couple who had been on the tour. They were from Melbourne. His name was Ty, and her name was Sarah. Given that I had spent the whole morning looking for Sarah at the Cascades Female Factory, it was appropriate.

Stitching 1

"That's a good counterpoint to the previous fire story," said Lilian. "This one is a phoenix story, the bird that rises from the ashes of destruction. The other story is about the strange aftermaths of surviving. It makes me think about the quiet, enduring effect of fire, and how this must affect many people in Tasmania still, as well as those who were in the Victorian fires."

"The reminders of the fires are built into the landscape, like those tall white ghosts I saw in the forests on the east coast of Bruny Island. Eventually they will disappear, but it will be many years yet."

"So, this is the last square? What now?"

"That was the last square. It's enough. It feels complete. But it would be nice to stitch it together."

"Of course it would. How would you like to proceed?"

"Being a writer, I would suggest that we start at the top left-hand corner, and go left to right, then move to the next line. And so on."

"Predictable, and pointless," responded Lilian.

"Yes, I know. I want it to be more than that. Even the stitches are important, even the thread. When I was at Cascades Female Factory, the guide was talking about the factory taking quotes for clothes that the convict women would make. There were two prices – one for where the materials and the cotton was supplied, and the other for where only the materials were supplied. Here was a situation where the thread carried its own price."

"Okay, so we will have due regard for the thread."

"Then there is the main thing – the design."

"We will have to meet," said Lilian, "now that you're back from your trip."

And so we met. Our meetings were usually irregular, perhaps once or twice a year. I don't think we were catching up; it was more like checking in. Neither of us felt that we were behind, but we were interested in what each other had been doing, what we were thinking about now, and how we were feeling.

Lilian was adept at quilting and she had a group of friends who met regularly and showed each other their work. Then they sewed together, just like the women of the *Rajah*. I had met her in an unrelated way. We had started up a conversation after an event. Someone had given a presentation about leadership and personal growth. They had an approach, a model, a language, and enthusiasm. Afterwards there was a mingling of the throng, and glasses of wine. People were talking about everything – the speakers' ideas, their own ideas, connections, experiences.

I noticed Lilian. She was wearing a pale blue blouse and a mid-green cotton skirt – distinctive, clear, but not bold. Her blonde hair flowed when she moved. She seemed confident, but without the need to dominate a group. We introduced themselves, and we talked about how the ideas that had been aired resonated with our own experience, while drinking a glass of wine.

We drifted away from the group. We said things that made each other laugh. That was a pleasant feeling. When Lilian laughed, her face illuminated and her hair waved gently around her. And there were moments of silence that were not uncomfortable.

After that we had resolved to meet. To what end? Just for the time that it was. And our store of shared experiences grew.

* * * * *

We met. We made tea. I covered the table in the study with pieces of paper.

"Good morning," I said.

We sat on the verandah. Lilian talked, while we looked at the garden and the pond.

"A quilt can be just a pretty pattern. It will have balance and repetition. You can play with light and dark, and colours, and lines and shapes."

"Okay, let's tick that off. I don't think I can reduce my squares to a mere pattern."

"Of course not, but one must set out the options. I have a question – what is 'the quilt approach'?"

"Ah, yes. I suppose it's my way of saying that life is not like a train. A train goes straight along the track until it gets to its destination. 'This train is going to Central' is not debatable, and there is nothing to be added or subtracted from that statement. But human lives, that is something else, and even a piece of a life, that is another story."

"Yes," said Lilian, "another story." I shrugged and smiled, thanking her for the acknowledgment of a very poor pun.

"At the same time," Lilian went on, "a quilt is not infinite. It is defined. It has a given length and breadth, and it has shapes within it – squares, for example."

"I am happy to accept the limitations," I replied.

"How are we going to do this?" she asked. "You can't just print out all the words on the quilt."

"Well, we could. Charlotte Bronte made tiny books when she was a girl, for toy soldiers to read. So, each of my squares could be rendered like a tiny book."

"The audience for the quilt will not be toy soldiers." Lilian was emphatic. "And the point of a quilt is to be visual."

"Yes, of course. That was the point of my train metaphor. The quilt should show that this piece of life that I have been writing about is not simply linear. There are ideas and themes that are involved, there are streams that run in parallel, and somehow it all makes sense."

"That's what I'm thinking. And even if it doesn't all make sense, there are events that point to one another and raise questions."

"But there is linear time," I pointed out. "Things occur in sequence, and you can't go back. We could put a timeline across the middle of the quilt, and put things above and below the line."

"No," said Lilian, "let's not do that. It puts all the emphasis on time, as if that were the main message of life. I don't think either of us thinks that."

I like Lilian. I could see, the first time I met her, that she knew how to say no when that was necessary.

"What if we have a timeline, as one element, and it goes all the way around the perimeter of the quilt?" I suggested. "That way, we accept that it is a real, conditioning factor in life, but inside this perimeter there are other themes."

And there we had it – a suggestion, an idea, that the quilt would have a border which would be a timeline.

"I have a question," Lilian said. "If a timeline goes all the way around, it comes back to itself. Does that imply that the beginning point and the end point are the same? You know, that lovely quote from T.S. Eliot: 'We shall not cease from exploration, and the end of all our exploring will be to arrive where we started and know the place for the first time.'"

"Yes, I like that. We're not saying that the beginning point and the end point are the same; we're not saying time is circular. But we are asking people (or tin soldiers) to look at the end point in the light of the beginning point, or vice versa. What do you think?"

"Sure, I like that. Now, what is this timeline? Where does it start and end?"

At this point it was necessary to make coffee. We hadn't yet got to the table of scattered papers. I made coffee and we got a big blank piece of paper instead. We ate nice biscuits with the coffee. Lilian drew a big rectangle on the sheet of paper.

"We are working with thirty-two squares," she said. "So, I have decided that the quilt will be eight squares by four squares, plus the border. Is that okay?"

"That's the quilt approach," I said, smiling.

"Now, let's talk about the timeline. What is the scope of it?"

I had been thinking. "I think the end point is easy enough – now, the end point of my latest trip to Tasmania. That seems like a sensible boundary. But the beginning? There is 1973, my trip to Tasmania then. But then there are the family history elements, and once I admit that into the picture, I have to think more broadly, about causes and contexts."

"What do you mean?"

"Well, for example, Sarah arrived in Hobart Town in 1850, but there is a background to consider – her crime and her trial, then there is her family, and there is the Irish potato famine."

"That could go on forever," Lilian argued gently.

"No, no. I can set a broad point that makes sense in terms of the subsequent stories. Let's say the starting point for the timeline is 1800. That takes in the Archers who came to Tasmania, and their jumping-off point in Hertfordshire. This also takes in my William Archer. He was born in 1813."

"And when were Edward and Sarah born?"

"Edward was born in 1829. Sarah was born somewhere between 1830 and 1833."

"Okay, that sets a context for us. The next thing is, there are four sides to a quilt. Can you break up your timeline into four parts?"

"Yes, I could do that. This is what I would suggest: 1800 to 1860; 1861 to 1920; 1921 to 1970; 1971 to 2020."

Lilian marked out a border around the big rectangle. She wrote the four sets of dates in the four sides of the border. She said, "It doesn't have to be a border, you know."

"What do you mean?"

"You could start with themes and make each of them a spiral that comes into the centre, which is now. There are three themes that I can see – your current trip to Tasmania, your trip to Tasmania in 1973, and the family history stream. What about that – three spirals that start on the outside and spiral in towards the centre in parallel?"

"That has possibilities. In that scenario, things from each of those streams of time all crash into the present and will either explode or fuse together. In some ways it was like that. Seeing the photos of the yards at Cascades Female Factory with the shafts of light coming down was like Sarah visiting me in the present. Or seeing that old house in Hobart and connecting it with the house I visited in 1973 was another collision. The spiral has merit."

"Let's go back to the timeline border. You split up the time frame into four periods. How do you see those four periods of time?"

"Across all four time periods, there is the backdrop of societies – the flow of social and political events and the growth of the colonies of Australia and Tasmania. There are the main factors in change, from the first period, when the Australian colonies were being established, through to Australia and Tasmania's evolving place in the world. Then there are the events in my family.

"By the end of that first period, 1800 to 1860, all of my ancestors had arrived in Australia. Edward Lewis arrived in Van Diemen's Land in 1845, Sarah Crosby arrived in 1850. My William Archer had arrived in New South Wales (as a convict) in 1838.

"I am interested in how Tasmania shows up in the sequence of events. In the first period, it shows up a lot. First, the miller's sons, the Archers, arrived and received large grants of land, which they built into very successful farms with the help of convict labour. In the same period, both Edward and Sarah were there as convicts. By 1860, the various strands of the Archer family in Tasmania had established both their wealth and their position in the colony. Edward and Sarah, on the other hand, had left, and were in Sydney.

"Somehow, the descendants of the William Archer in New South Wales (another of my great great grandfathers) knew about their southern cousins, but as far as I know, there was no contact between them. All of the other strands of my family settled on the mainland – South Australia, Victoria and New South Wales. No descendants of Edward and Sarah had anything to do with Tasmania. In fact, in 1897, when Sarah Lewis died, her death certificate said she had never been there at all; it said she was born in Ireland and had lived in South Australia, Victoria and New South Wales – Tasmania was erased.

"When I went to Tasmania in 1973, it was because my sister was getting married; she had been working as a nurse in Hobart. None of us knew any family history, so we didn't know that our great great grandparents had been convicts in Hobart, and that some of their children had been born there as well. Those were still the days when to have ancestors who were convicts was shameful. We grew up not having to wear that shame. All our ancestors were decent and respectable, as we supposed at the time.

"It wasn't until about 2013 that I started to explore family history, and it wasn't until about three years after that that I finally discovered my Tasmanian ancestors, Edward and Sarah Lewis. It was even more recently when I went digging for the Archers of Tasmania.

"If I think about this timeline as going in a big circle from 1800 to today, then it's like T.S. Eliot's quote – I am coming back to 1800 and seeing it for the first time. All the history I knew before was textbook knowledge. Now I have to see my ancestors, particularly Edward and Sarah, as people I know in those contexts. It was my Sarah who was a hungry child in the potato famine, on her own in London and fearful that she would die. It was my Edward who was a child pickpocket in London a few years earlier, staving off starvation through the use of his wits."

Lilian had listened attentively. "Well, it seems that you have a feel for the border as a timeline. It's a big span that goes for more than 200 years, and it circles back to its beginning. You could, for example, think about this in terms of the social conditions that formed Sarah's young life in Ireland, and ask, what is different about the social conditions between now and then. What has changed? How different are we? How different is our society?"

"Yes, I can do that for all of the people who have turned up in the squares, and look at what's different between them as well. It's a rich perspective."

Lilian was drawing again, scribbling notes and sketching shapes at various points around the big rectangle. While she was focused on that, I put the kettle on.

Stitching 2

Lilian and I swapped quilt ideas. I showed her the quilts I had seen in Tasmania, including the metal replica in the grounds of Cascades Female Factory. She showed me quilts that she had made, and quilts by other people she knew. Looking at each one was like looking at a world. It was different from looking at a painting.

Quilts gave you a sense that pattern and structure are part of the intent. They made me think of the yantra as an analogy. A yantra is a diagram generally associated with Hinduism, and generally based on the form of a square as the outside frame. It can incorporate triangles, lotus leaves and circles arranged in concentric circles that bring your eye into the centre.

A yantra may be referred to as a 'mystical' diagram with secret powers. I don't find talk like that helpful. What I do find helpful is the idea that reality has pattern and structure and movement. And why does it? Because life is the result of tensions between different forces. It's as simple as this: the temperature today is a result of the tension between hot and cold. There are forces at play, and we are always in the centre, and there is always a balance being struck. And it is always moving, changing.

Or, the balance is between love, hate and indifference. And in the midst of this, we can decide which fire to feed.

"How do you want to proceed?" asked Lilian. I don't know how much we said; the conversation just seemed to go on.

"I had thought about putting the extracts from the 1973 diary into another border inside the timeline border," I said.

"I understand why you would want to do that," she answered, "but it's not the best idea."

"Why?" Again, Lilian is confident.

"It's about simple geometry. I know you want to do it because it's the next thing that comes up, and the movement is through time towards the centre of the quilt, where you want to end up. But the simple truth is that this border would be much bigger than the one inside it. As you approach the centre, you have less space to play with, and you will probably want the opposite!"

It was obvious when you thought about it. I was stumped. But the analogy of the yantra rescued me. It was the gateway. "I want to depict the past and the present as the tension between conflicting forces, or, the temporary resolution of the tension between two forces. That will be the centrepiece of the quilt, and we will fill that concept out with the stories I have written. That gives us three perspectives – the trip I just went on, the 1973 trip, and the figures from my family history."

Lilian groaned. I took the opportunity to make tea and bring something nice to eat. "Perhaps we should dance," I said.

She was not to be distracted. "We have to think about how this can be represented visually. Remember the exhibit you told me about from MONA? The one with the room piled up with stacks of glass or slate, not inexplicable, but depressing? We have to take care that we don't end up like that, and all covered with dust that is the most depressing grey you can think of."

"Okay," I said. "I will try. We agree that there are three elements – the current trip, the 1973 trip, and the family history. That's a triangle. That's in the yantra. We've got to be able to work with this."

"Alright," said Lilian. "Let's test it out. Let's take something that happened."

"Okay. Here's something. I want to start with Edward Lewis. He is my great great grandfather, so one-sixteenth of me is him. I know he was sent to Hobart, in 1845, as a boy of about fifteen. After my recent trip to Tasmania, I wonder if he was sent to Point Puer across the water from Port Arthur. If so, he would have been sent back to Hobart in 1847, because Point Puer was closed. And the boys were sent to a yard which was attached to Cascades Female Factory.

"So, he could have been there when Sarah arrived in 1850, and he could have been the man who was found in her bed there in July 1850. He would have been about twenty, and she about seventeen.

He could have been the father of the child that Sarah had in 1851, before their marriage in 1853 – the child Mary Ann Crosby. I made inquiries about her on my trip to Tasmania, but I found nothing."

"Where are you going with this?" asked Lilian.

"I'm getting there," I replied. "So, when I went to Hobart in 1973, I went there with no knowledge of my family history. All I had was the prejudices I grew up with, which included the idea that I had no connection with convicts, and, from my Anglican upbringing, the view that sex was something that should never occur outside of marriage. And then, when I came back in 2019, all of that had changed. I was connected with convicts, and two of them may have had a relationship before they married. There may have even been a child of that relationship."

"Do you think that is true?" said Lilian, before quickly realising I was presenting the unprovable but possible turn of events.

"Yes," I said. "At least, that is what is at play."

Lilian sketched rapidly with her pencil. I don't know what she was sketching, but she was intent on it.

Stitching 3

"When I was in Hobart in 1973," I began.

"Okay, let's start there," Lilian replied. "I have to get more of a sense of how we work through the three points of the triangle."

"But perhaps I will not help you with that," I said. "Not with this story. This story has no family history in it. But let it be said anyway. It was New Year, remember? And we had had an ecstatic night, and we know that an ecstatic New Year's Eve is the culmination of a full year of experiences. And at midnight, among the jubilant throng was an older man who was wearing an RSL badge, and he was hugged as one of us, in the lightness of the moment. But behind all that, for him, were the memories of the horrors of the Second World War, whether they were his personal memories or stories that had been shared with him down at the RSL club – the barbaric Japanese who tortured and starved people, fellow humans, and worked them to death.

"What did any of us think about that at the time? How did we reconcile those stories with the post-war reality that we had grown up in, the idea that we had to go on, we had to aim to make a friendly world? And this in the middle of the irony of the Cold War, the idea that, simultaneously, we believed in doom."

"The contrast, for me, was seeing the Japanese garden at the Royal Tasmanian Botanical Gardens this year. It had not been there in 1973. It was constructed in 1987."

"That's not something that was in your stories."

"No matter; it happened. And the garden has had over thirty years to grow. It was beautiful. It was spring, so everything was in bloom, and it was gorgeous. There were all the classic features you would expect: stone lanterns, maple trees, bridges, walkways over the water, waterfalls, rocks, and everything was positioned so beautifully. It is perhaps the best Japanese garden I have ever seen, although one does not like to fall into comparisons. Let's just say it was perfect.

"The question is, can these be the same people who treated prisoners of war so dreadfully, so callously?"

"And what do you think?" asked Lilian.

"I think they are not. I think gardeners are not apparatchiks. They are not the people who will do anything at all to fulfil the ends of war, or the ends of their masters. Our aged ex-soldiers will tell us this, the returned soldiers who are now close to one hundred years old, who are so frail, but who remember so vividly, man massacring man, and women and children too. Finally, they say, it was all abominably wrong. And a Japanese garden is exalted. It is not a victory statement. It is the alternative statement, the affirmation of the necessity of gentleness and humility."

"You want that in the quilt as well?" asked Lilian, and her eyes were wide.

"I do," I said. "Somewhere between 1973 and 1987, in Tasmania, something happened to allow this to be said. I know it happened elsewhere as well, but it helps to focus on a particular place, because shifts like this have to happen specifically. They don't happen generically."

"When I was in Hobart in 1973," I began again.

Lilian had been quiet. She still had a sketchpad lying on the table near her. We had walked over to my table with a pile of squares on it representing all the stories I had written, but we needed to think visually, so we came back to the table on the verandah.

"Yes," she said, "when you were in Hobart..."

"There was the question of what work I would do when I went home, and that's a theme."

"How is it a theme?"

"Because it's part of everyone's life. You have to choose it, or accept the work that you enter, and then spend your life doing it. In 1973, the people I was travelling with were all young adults, and we were all wrestling with the question of what work we would do. For most of us, the question was, what work would we spend our lives doing? Olga had just finished a social work degree, and she was thinking about whether that's what she really wanted to do. She and Donna were working in a restaurant. That was only temporary. Paul was talking about not pursuing a career, but building a log cabin in the bush."

"And what were you doing?"

"Good question. I was thinking about it. I had had most of the year off work, and I had only been back teaching for a couple of months. I wanted to get out and do something else. So, Tasmania for me was a chance to be somewhere else other than home so I could think about it."

"And what did you do when you went home?"

"I resigned from teaching. I went back to university full-time, but within three months I had quit from that and got a job as a psychiatric nurse. I did that for six months and then left Sydney and went to Queensland."

"So, Tasmania shook things up for you as far as work was concerned?"

"Yes, I think it was significant. I needed to shake things up, or I would have stayed in teaching and not really been committed to it. As it was, I eventually found my direction. It took a couple of decades, but it all seemed to be necessary."

"Okay, so, when you came back to Tasmania recently, how did you stand in relation to work then?"

"It was timely, because I had left my job earlier in the year. I hadn't left in an irrevocable way, but I did leave my job, and I haven't been back. That means, I am standing here now looking back at 1973 in terms of a lifetime of work that I have done. Although it has been a zigzag path, I feel that I have done some worthwhile things."

"Okay, and then there is the question of how you see family history in terms of people and their lifetimes of work."

"I will focus on Edward Lewis first, because, like me, his path was not straightforward. His career started as a boy in London, making a living by picking people's pockets and dealing in stolen goods. I put this down to the need to survive. As a convict, I don't know what he did. He could have been at Point Puer, but most of the boys there learned a trade, and Edward doesn't seem to have done that.

"But, Edward did know how to read and write, and that may have marked him out for administrative jobs. After he finished his sentence as a convict, he became a special constable for the police. Soon after, he became a detective in Sydney. That led to some tumultuous episodes, and after this he became a legal clerk. There is a lot of evidence that he later went back into the police force and spent another twenty years as a policeman and detective again."

"That was quite a zigzag path, then," Lilian commented, "like yours."

"Yes," I said, "and then there are the Tasmanian Archers."

"What would you say about them?"

"There are many different stories there, but I would focus on the Archers at Brickendon, and the impression I get from them that there is a continuity of the practice of farming over six or seven generations. There is a steadiness in that, and there seems to be an awareness of the need to always be ready to innovate, to change, and to treat the land kindly. And I liked their house garden, and the fact that they have kept the very first, modest cottage that was built on the farm, that their first William Archer had lived in when he first went there."

Lilian was writing notes and sketching. I had no idea how the many things I had talked about could be captured and expressed in images, but I trusted there was a way.

Stitching 4

I said to Lilian, "When people heard that I was going to Tasmania, the first question they asked me was whether I had been there before. When I told them the answer was once, and it was in 1973, they all said that was great. When I came back, the question they asked was, how different was it from the first time?"

"And what was your answer to that question?" smiled Lilian.

"Some things I recalled, because they were the same, and some things were brand new. And some things had been scrubbed up to look new."

"But what was your impression of the change?"

"When I went to Hobart in 1973, there were lots of old buildings: old, charming stone buildings."

"They are still there, aren't they?"

"Yes, much more so than in Sydney, or any other Australian city I've been in. There are new buildings, too. You'd have to expect that after forty-six years. But there is also the move towards tokenism, merely using the past for effect. There was a construction site near Salamanca Markets where an entire building had been destroyed, except for this – one façade had been retained. The façade had nothing behind it, and it was held upright with a steel frame that was bigger than the wall itself. What will come is a completely new building that purports to preserve the charm of the past. One assumes they will remove the steel frame."

"That's just one instance," Lilian tried to argue.

"Some things are true symbolically. That one instance could be symbolic of how we see the past generally. We can accept snapshots of it, and there is something in us that hankers for connection to the

152

past. The façade was a snapshot. But the judgement is that the past is not functional compared with today, so it has to go. Ironically, the preservation of that façade is likewise telling us that the modern building is not going to give us what we get from the past, which we could call charm."

"Charm?" said Lilian.

"A charm is a spell or an incantation. We are beguiled by these buildings of the past. They suggest to us something more about humans than mere bricks and mortar. For contrast, I went to a place where the buildings were all new. You could tell that the new buildings were intended to be interesting. But they weren't. Putting a wall out at a weird angle doesn't make a building interesting. Painting bits of it in garish paint doesn't either."

"But not all old buildings are interesting."

"A lot of old buildings were really aesthetic, and were built with a lot of effort and skill. Today we create buildings quickly and cheaply, using mass processes. They are built to serve a function, and it doesn't seem to matter if the function is only temporary. They can be knocked down again. Aesthetics doesn't come into it, or if it does, the aim is generally to display cleverness or to be shocking."

"Well," asked Lilian, "are we talking about buildings?"

"Not as such; I think we are talking about the inexorable march of progress, and the values we have exchanged in that march. You realise I am using the word 'progress' ironically?"

"Yes, I do," said Lilian, drolly. "But if we are talking about the past, how do you separate the good and the bad? Isn't the point of the Cascades Female Factory site, for example, to highlight what was undesirable about the past? You could even say it is there to remind us not to conduct ourselves like that ever again."

"Or, we simply need something to distract us from the emptiness of the present. Anything will do, but curiously, the past has a strong pull on us. The trouble today is that the past has been vilified; it is the place where all the mistakes were made. But maybe the past judges the present too. Consider the buildings."

"Okay, I am understanding it now," said Lilian, "in terms of a tension between the past and present. Maybe we are, collectively, falling into the trap of thinking the present is good and the past is bad and that, as The Beatles said, 'It's getting better all the time'."

"If you can say it clearly like that, you will be able to design the quilt!" I said, excitedly. "Of course, we don't know if The Beatles were being ironic or not."

"I don't think they were," Lilian replied. "They say 'I have to admit', which suggests they were at first unwilling to accept that things were getting better. On the other hand, we could say that things were only getting better in 1967."

"I don't want to get lost in generalities," I said. "I'm interested in the forces at play that give rise to the present. What troubles me is that the forces that hold sway are those that overrun the natural world and cover it with the expanding city. I can use the words of another song, a Beachboys song called 'Californian Saga': 'Humanity has multiplied, their powers are enlarged, their powers and follies have become fantastic'. This is it – humanity's powers have become fantastic, and at the same time, so have our follies."

"But don't we have to look to the future?" asked Lilian. "I don't believe this, but I'm saying it because that's what people say." She smiled. Irony was in the air today.

"This is what I've got to say about that. We have nothing to take to the future unless we look at the past – what has been done already, and what has been done before. Otherwise all we have is just trite nonsense. But looking at the past can also be trite nonsense, if it is just to say, well, we don't flog people anymore.

"I think the question to ask about the past is, where are the noble souls? That's what we need to find. And even if the best people we find are flawed, we ask of them – what is it about them that had a noble intention? And whatever is flawed, we ask, how could we do that better? And that is what we need to bring with us into the future."

"Okay," said Lilian, "I can see that as a theme, and I will look for that in your stories. Is there more to come?"

"Yes, there is more, a little more."

"Okay." Lilian was writing more notes, and sketching. The space within the outside border of the rectangle was becoming populated. A quilt was in the flux of creation. I thought of the steel-framed quilt in the yard at Cascades Female Factory.

Stitching 5

I said to Lilian, "There is something more that needs to be said about Aborigines, and I want it to be part of the centre, the active part. When I was in Tasmania in 1973, there was no sign of Aborigines. They were considered to belong to the past. In any case, no one seemed to know how they could be part of the present. Their lifestyle was gone, and it was incompatible with the western way of life."

"Let's have some tea and talk about it," said Lilian. "It needs talk."

"This time when I went to Tasmania, there was recognition of Aborigines. There was even recognition of the dark days of the Black War in the 1820s and 1830s when Aborigines could be shot and killed, even women and children, and an army of the settlers marched right across the island to round up the Aborigines and banish them to Flinders Island."

"Yes, but now it is recognised that there are people who are descendants of the Aboriginal peoples," Lilian said.

"True, but I think the main idea that is still held about the British settlers is that they brought modern civilisation, including productive agriculture and mining, and these are what made the colony successful. But it seems to me that much of what they did was plundering. Just to take the example of the place I visited, Mount Bischoff – tin was discovered and it was mined until it was all gone. This was true of any ore that the British colonists found; they took everything they could find until it was all gone. And this is still true.

"The same approach applied to trees. Any trees that provided useful timber and were accessible were logged as far as they could be. There was little thought given to the sustainability of timber until the mid-twentieth century, and there was no thought given to the effects of chopping down trees on the locality – say, the effects on erosion, wildlife or rivers.

"What happened with agriculture? There has certainly been productive agriculture, but the thing to be said about that is that it was done by conquest, not by working with the environment as they found it. At the Archer properties, for example, the native grasses were replaced by introduced grasses and the area took on the look of an English pastoral scene. The Australian native animals were displaced just as definitely as were the Aborigines."

"You are saying that our society is not sustainable?" asked Lilian.

"Our society is not at all sustainable, and there is still no serious notion of pursuing that goal. Since the time the British colonies commenced in Van Diemen's Land and Sydney, the settlers have used up what is there and gone looking for the next thing to use up. It's an obvious issue: if you use something up, one day it will be gone, and what will you do then? This is such a deep attitude. You would have to go back to the eighteenth century, before the industrial revolution, to find people who didn't rely on finding something new from somewhere else to use up in order to maintain their way of life."

"But," said Lilian, "wouldn't critics say that the whole point of modern methods is that they add value, so we are better off?"

"Yes, that's exactly what they would say," I replied. "My response would be that it doesn't matter. That's just an argument about money, and if your society is not sustainable, eventually it will fail."

"Your critics would say that that's a problem for the future, and we are very clever as a species, and we will solve that problem then, as we have always done."

"I would say that that is an argument that was formed when there were still lands to conquer. It's also an argument that admits the truth of what it opposes – the way our society operates is not sustainable. And I say that this is immoral. It is immoral in terms of indigenous law, not just in Australia, but all around the world."

"You used the word 'law' when you talked about the Boy Scouts. And Aborigines talk about law in relation to land," Lilian observed.

"Our British past doesn't allow us to understand this. The British think the law is something that is made in parliaments. I think the law is in us, and the central principle of the law is sustainability. And the measure of that is, not ten years or fifty years, but the lifetime of the planet."

"You brought up this issue in relation to Aborigines?" queried Lilian.

"It is the next step. It's one thing to recognise Aborigines, and to recognise that our British ancestors displaced them from their lands, killed them, brutalised them, banished them and looked down on them. The deeper lesson is that their way of life was sustainable, and ours isn't. Our society has developed over a little more than 200 years and has been based on conquest and plundering the land. Their society existed for longer than any other societies on the planet, and it was a viable society when our ancestors arrived. They knew the law. We have to learn it.

"If we knew the law, our quilt would be about the seasons and the weather, the movements of birds and animals, and the movements of the stars. It would be about what to do in days to come, and how to dance our gratitude for the bounty of the earth."

Lilian took a new page in her sketchbook and began to draw.

Stitching 6

Lilian and I met again after a few days. She asked me how I was, and I asked her the same. We were both okay. We both had a lot on our minds.

I said, just to start the conversation: "I know it's hard to render ideas visually. I decided when I was five not to do it. When I showed a drawing from school to my mother, she told me all my heads looked like squares, so I decided to concentrate on words instead."

"You may have been yearning to make a patchwork quilt," she quipped.

"I had not thought of that possibility," I replied. "After doing art class in high school, I thought I may have been a Cubist."

Lilian brought the conversation around to quilts. "I think I can do it," she said. "The quilt will have squares, or panels, or patches, as we sometimes call them, and there will also be stitching over the top so I can incorporate some triangles into the design, and I will try to evoke the idea of the yantra. I know you want that."

I began talking. "Yes, that's great. I must say, I got distracted by the idea of Charlotte Bronte's tiny books, and then I started to picture every square in the quilt as a tiny book."

"Banish that thought!" said Lilian. "Some things are just not possible in a given medium. Or wise," she added.

"I was going through my photos again, and I found something I liked."

"We can't add anything else!" Lilian protested.

"No, no. This was just for my satisfaction and yours. My views about current mindsets in society might be seen as harsh, but these are generalised views, things I think need to be said. Within that, people hold many different views, and some of them I can relate to closely. When I was in the Royal Tasmanian Botanical Gardens in Hobart, I came across a sculpture. It looked like a big cauldron, the kind you see in Chinese culture.

"The sculpture was called 'Blue Gum', and it was made by Marcus Tatton out of big chunks of blue gum. It was the inscription I wanted to share with you. It said: 'This sculpture symbolises reverence for the great forests of blue gums in Tasmania which we all inherit when we come to live in this unique part of the world.'"

"That's the law!" said Lilian.

"Yes," I said quietly, "that's the law in somebody's heart."

Lilian held up a sketch for me. I liked it. It contained surprises, but I could also see how she had incorporated ideas that we had talked about.

I got excited again. "I have this idea that every moment that comes into being is the result of forces that are striving for expression – good and bad, if you like, or, Heaven is contending with Earth. And that is happening every moment, so there is constant change. In the best of situations, it is the good that is striving for expression, but it is nearly always imperfect. We don't get it quite right, but we keep practising, as dancers do. The thought of perfection becomes the reality of imperfection, and then we try again. This is what makes noble souls."

Lilian smiled. "I never promised you a perfect quilt," she said, "but I will try and incorporate that thought into it. Now, don't talk anymore!"

And I didn't. I was happy.

* * * * *

Author's Note

This book is clearly based on true events. I don't deny it. Fiction has its delights and amusement, but reality is more compelling.

Though I go to you
ceaselessly along dream paths,
the sum of those trysts
is less than a single glimpse
granted in the waking world.

(Ono No Komachi, c. 825-900)

I admit to moments of fiction within these pages, but only in the spirit of the whole. If you knew, you would forgive me, I am sure. I admit also that Lilian is a fiction. I did invent her, although I can say there is sufficient material in my life for her to have been stitched together credibly.

Enjoy.

www.ingramcontent.com/pod-product-compliance
Lightning Source LLC
Chambersburg PA
CBHW031113260626
47172CB00001B/345